THE REGULATOR SERIES, BOOK 2

MURPHY'S LAW

ETHAN J. WOLFE

THORNDIKE PRESS

A part of Gale, Cengage Learning

GALE
CENGAGE Learning·

Farmington Hills, Mich • San Francisco • New York • Waterville, Maine
Meriden, Conn • Mason, Ohio • Chicago

GALE
CENGAGE Learning®

LIBRARY OF CONGRESS CATALOGING-IN-PUBLICATION DATA

Names: Wolfe, Ethan J., author.
Title: Murphy's law / by Ethan J. Wolfe.
Description: Large print edition. | Waterville, Maine : Thorndike Press, 2016. |
    © 2015 | Series: Thorndike Press large print western | Series: The Regulator
    series ; book 2
Identifiers: LCCN 2016003776| ISBN 9781410488695 (hardcover) | ISBN 1410488691
    (hardcover)
Subjects: LCSH: Counterfeits and counterfeiting—United States—Fiction. | United
    States—History—Civil War, 1861-1865—Veterans—Fiction. | Large type books. |
    GSAFD: Western stories. | Historical fiction. | Mystery fiction.
Classification: LCC PS3612.A5433 M87 2016 | DDC 813/.6—dc23
LC record available at http://lccn.loc.gov/2016003776

Published in 2016 by arrangement with Ethan J. Wolfe

Printed in Mexico
1 2 3 4 5 6 7 20 19 18 17 16

MURPHY'S LAW

enjoyed the solitude having the land provided him. And now Sally, as she thrived on the solitude.

The plan was to sell the farm and move south to his home in Tennessee, and if Burke still wanted him on staff, to have a telegraph installed in the home for quick communications.

When he turned off the road to the long path that led to the house, Sally was riding the small bay he gave her for her birthday last month. She named the bay Misty because the first time she rode her there was a fine mist of rain in the air.

Murphy rode out to the north field to meet her and they dismounted by the small stream that ran through the property.

They sat beside the stream under the shade of a tall tree.

"Do we have a new president?" Sally asked.

"Sworn in before I left."

Sally's blond hair was pinned up and her face was void of the makeup she wore when in the railroad camp. She was thirty-six, but appeared a decade younger, even in the bright sunlight.

"Are you going to the inaugural ball?" Sally asked.

"I'm not much for parties," Murphy said.

11

Sally hated going into Washington for the fear of being recognized. Imagining some congressman or senator recognizing her at the president's inaugural ball. Wouldn't that make great conversation at staff meetings?

"Burke is coming by around seven," Murphy said. "He said he had something he needs to discuss with me."

"By coincidence I have an extra hen to go into the oven," Sally said.

"Want to finish your ride?" Murphy asked, as he stood up.

"Let's do," Sally said.

Murphy guided Sally back onto the saddle, then he mounted Boyle and they rode to the end of the north field and then turned south. The afternoon sun was hot and they kept the horses' pace to a slow gait.

When they reached the house, Sally said, "Have I time for a bath?"

"I'll tend the horses and set the water to boiling," Murphy said.

Sally kissed him lightly on the lips. She had to stand on her toes just to reach his chin, so he bent a little to meet her lips. "The tub is big enough for two."

"I'll boil extra water then," Murphy said.

Murphy looked at Sally as she washed her

hair with liquid hair soap that came in a glass bottle like soda pop. Murphy used the bar of harsh soap to wash his hair, but slowly he was adapting to her ways. The shampoo was just one of the many feminine items she took with her when she left Saint Louis, where she took as many as six baths a week.

Just watching her wash her hair stirred him.

She rinsed the soap by dunking under the water.

"Do you know what Mr. Burke wants?" Sally asked, as she squeezed her hair with her hands.

"No."

"An assignment?"

"Possibly."

"Your father is expecting us in the fall."

"I know."

"I don't want to live in Washington."

"You're worried about nothing, but I agree with you," Murphy said. "I'm sick of Washington politics myself."

"And now that I've retired from my profession, I would like to be an honest woman," Sally said.

"Who will give you away?" Murphy asked.

"How about your father?"

"We can ask him when we go south. I'm

sure he will be proud to walk you down the aisle."

"What about this place?" Sally said. "All this land wasted."

"I was thinking of sharecropping it out after we leave instead of selling it," Murphy said. "Let it earn a bit of money for us."

Sally stared at Murphy for a few seconds and he thought he saw a mist form in her eyes and he wondered if he said something that upset her.

"What is it?" he asked.

"Us." Sally shook her head. "You said 'us.' "

And so he did.

Chapter Two

Burke arrived by chauffeur-driven carriage. The carriage was reserved for the vice-president, but as Arthur was now president and would use the carriage reserved for his new office, why let it go to waste?

Murphy met him on the porch.

"Your man want some supper?" Murphy asked. "There's plenty."

Burke looked at the driver. "I've tasted her cooking. She's pretty good."

"Why not?" the driver said.

"After dinner you wait for me in the carriage," Burke said. "And grab my case."

Sally met them in the dining room. She wore a simple yellow dress with her hair pinned up in a bun. Burke thought her a striking-looking woman.

"This is my driver, Mr. Christopher," Burke said.

Sally nodded politely to Christopher.

"Nice to meet you," Christopher said.

"Miss Sally."

Sally thought she detected just a hint of sarcasm in Christopher's voice, but she dismissed it as being slightly paranoid.

"Let's eat first," Murphy said. "We'll talk business later."

Burke set his case on the desk in the parlor and looked at Sally. She was pouring coffee. "Would you excuse us for a bit, Sally?" he said.

Murphy was stuffing his pipe and looked at Burke. "She can stay if she has a mind to," he said. "Save me the trouble of telling her about it later."

Burke didn't approve, but there was no use arguing with Murphy. The man answered only to his own conscience. "Understand that this is highly classified and can not leave this room," Burke said.

Sally set the coffee pot on the desk, nodded to Burke, and took a chair against the wall. "Who would I tell?" she said.

Burke opened the case and dumped the contents onto the desk.

Murphy looked at the stacks of money. Five-, ten-, and twenty-dollar bills bound with US Treasury paper strips.

"Grab a stack and tell me what you see," Burke said.

Murphy picked up a stack of five-dollar bills and removed one. He rubbed his thumb and finger across the bill and said, "Counterfeit."

"That's right," Burke said.

Sally leaned forward in her chair. "You mean that's fake money?"

Murphy nodded. "All of it," he said.

"How can you tell so quickly?" Sally said.

"One of the primary functions of the Secret Service is detection and prevention of counterfeit money," Burke said.

"But, how can you tell?" Sally asked again.

"Paper's too thick and this bill is made from real paper," Murphy said. "The art work is good, real good. A master forger designed the plates, but the government uses special paper that is made from cotton and linen fibers. Cotton and linen are waterproof so the bills aren't ruined when wet. Paper also burns much quicker and uneven."

Murphy touched the bill to the flame of the oil lamp and it ignited quickly and burst into flames. He set it in the ashtray on the desk and it was ash within seconds.

Murphy removed a twenty from a stack and held it to the light of the oil lamp.

"Damn fine work," Murphy said. "Who made this?"

"We don't know," Burke said.

Sally stood up. "Can I see?"

Murphy handed her the bill.

"What do you mean it's too thick?" Sally said.

"The press at the Treasury uses enormous pressure to compact the sheets of money before cutting," Murphy said.

"For the past several months, banks and stores all across the west have taken in thousands of bills just like these," Burke said. "That's where most of these bills came from. Garfield was working with the Treasury to determine where the source of the bills is when, well, you know. He was going to call you in two months ago after you finished up the serial killer business and now Arthur has asked me to assign you to the task. Quietly, of course. We don't want to panic the nation and especially the Wall Street bankers."

"Look at my fingers," Sally said.

"The ink never quite dries right," Murphy said. "They can figure out the color scheme, but never the exact formula for the ink. The special ink takes better to the cotton, linen fibers than straight paper."

Sally wiped her fingers on her apron. "Why go to all this trouble if banks and such can spot the fake money right off?"

she asked.

Burke looked at Murphy.

"More can't than can," Murphy said. "Enough of this stuff gets circulated it hurts Wall Street and causes panic in the market. Stocks fall and the economy takes a hit like after the war."

"Murphy, this stuff is turning up overseas," Burke said.

Murphy struck a match and lit his pipe. "Where?"

"Europe. Germany, France, a few other places."

"UK?" Murphy said.

"Not yet. The potential is disaster if allowed to grow," Burke said.

"I don't understand," Sally said.

"Right now the US ranks fifth in world economy," Burke said. "We are the growing giant in the room. By nineteen hundred we will rank second only to Great Britain. A major hit to us right now could cause a recession and even a depression and upset the world economic powers. A new world giant could emerge and that giant might not believe in the freedoms that we do."

Sally looked at the stack of bills.

"All that from some fake money?" she said.

"Enough of it in circulation, yes," Burke said.

"Coin?" Murphy asked.

"None as far as we know. Too heavy to transport is my guess," Burke said.

"Have you a list of areas where the money has been identified?" Murphy said.

"Almost complete," Burke said. "I should have it by late tomorrow."

Murphy sucked on his pipe and filled the air with sweet-smelling smoke.

"I want something in return," he said.

"I'm prepared to double your regular fee on this one," Burke said.

"Besides that," Murphy said. "A personal favor from you."

"If I can."

"Escort Sally to my farm in Tennessee," Murphy said. "We're going to rent this farm to sharecroppers and I'll work out of the Tennessee location. I want you to authorize a telegraph instillation built in the house for me to use. Okay?"

"No use saying no," Burke said.

Burke looked at Sally.

"When do you want to leave?"

"Two weeks okay?" Sally asked.

"Fine," Burke said. "I'll be back tomorrow late afternoon. Take samples of the money to bring on the trip."

Murphy sat on the porch swinging chairs and waited for Sally to come out with mugs of coffee.

The night air was sweet with the smell of blossoms from the bushes around the house and of coffee from the pot boiling inside on the stove.

He pulled out his pouch and stuffed his pipe with fresh tobacco and lit it with a wood match. Sally pushed open the screen door and came out with two mugs of coffee and gave him one.

She took a seat next to Murphy and the swinging chair rocked a bit.

"How long do you figure to be gone?" Sally asked.

"Hard to figure until I have a chance to get a feel for things."

"A month?"

"Maybe. Maybe less."

"Maybe more?"

"Possibly."

Sally sipped some coffee from her mug. "Anything from here you want moved?"

"Most of my clothes. Anything you want from the kitchen. My gun safe. The house in Tennessee is well furnished, but we can

21

buy anything new that you want," Murphy said.

"What I want is you," Sally said.

"As busy as you're going to be you won't hardly notice I'm gone."

"Maybe during the day, but I get into a cold, empty bed at night I'll notice you're not there," Sally said.

Murphy sipped some coffee and then sucked on his pipe.

"Promise me two things," Sally said. "That you won't get killed out there and you'll stay true blue."

"I will do my absolute best not to get killed," Murphy said. "And you need not worry about me staying true blue."

"I'm sure that every man with a wife and kids at home who visited my brothel told his wife he was true blue," Sally said.

"You have my word," Murphy said. "I can spit on your hand and we can shake to seal the promise if you'd like."

"I have a better way to seal that promise," Sally said.

"Oh?"

"Finish your coffee first," Sally said.

CHAPTER THREE

Murphy sat on a hardback chair and scanned the long list given to him by Burke. Next to him, Burke sipped the cold lemonade Sally had brought out to the porch.

Christopher waited in the carriage. "I was wondering, Mr. Murphy, if I could trouble Miss Sally for a glass of that lemonade," he asked.

"Hey, Sally, could I trouble you for another glass of lemonade for Burke's driver?" Murphy said.

"When will you leave?" Burke asked. "The president is anxious to find the source and put an end to this before it becomes too widely known."

"Tomorrow morning," Murphy said.

Sally opened the screen door and stepped out to the porch. She looked at Christopher, who grinned at her.

"Nothing east of Topeka, it seems according to your list," Murphy said. "Denver was hard hit. I'll start there and move around according to the leads."

Sally walked down the porch steps and handed the glass to Christopher. He placed his hand over hers and held it tightly for a moment and grinned. "Thank you, ma'am," he said and released his grip.

"I'll tell the president your plans," Burke said.

Sally turned away from Christopher and walked up the steps and stood behind Murphy.

Burke stood up, as did Murphy, and they shook hands.

"Good luck," Burke said.

Burke walked down the steps to the carriage and climbed into the back seat.

Christopher touched his hat and looked at Sally. "Thank you for the drink, ma'am," he said and set the empty glass on the hitching post. "Hope to see you again soon."

Murphy laid out two sets of black trail clothes, underwear, socks, and toiletries on the bed. Everything would fit inside the lone satchel he would bring on the trip west.

While Sally cooked supper, he unlocked the gun safe in the closet and thought about his choice of weapons. He wouldn't be hunting a crazed serial killer on this trip and he liked to match his weapons according to the particular assignment.

He selected a Winchester 73 carbine rifle chambered in .44-40 ammunition. The carbine model had a twenty-inch-long barrel for ease of portability and a 15-round, tubular magazine.

He tossed the rifle and several boxes of ammunition onto the bed.

For a sidearm he selected a Colt Peacemaker revolver chambered in .44-40 ammunition so that he needn't carry more than one type on the trip. The five-and-a-half-inch barrel made the revolver a quicker draw than the seven-and-three-quarters-inch Schofield if the need arose. The trigger pull had been reduced by a gunsmith at his request and when fanned, the weapon could fire six rounds in mere seconds. He placed it into a slick, black leather holster. The gun belt also held an eight-inch knife for trail use and he tossed it on the bed.

Satisfied with his weapons, Murphy closed and locked the safe and went into the kitchen where Sally was making fried chicken at the stove. He kissed the back of her neck and then filled a glass with cool lemonade and sat at the table.

"Everything will be ready in ten minutes," Sally said. "It's a lovely evening; would you like to eat outside at the table out back?"

"I believe I would," Murphy said.

The table faced west and they ate the evening meal with a view of the setting sun.

"I think I would like to have a dog," Sally said.

"A dog?"

"They're a fine companion, especially when you're away."

"What kind of dog?"

"The few times we've visited Washington I've seen women with tiny lap dogs and they look ridiculous," Sally said. "What kind of protection are they?"

"Burke has a pair of Great Danes," Murphy said. "He'll see me off in the morning. I could ask him about them and he'll come see you about it."

"Yes, that would be good," Sally said.

"Speaking of protection, can you handle a shotgun?" Murphy said.

"I never have," Sally said. "I have fired a .32 pistol. I always kept one on me for protection."

"A .32 won't do you much good against an attacker unless he agrees to stand still and lets you shoot him in the head from point-blank range," Murphy said. "I'll leave you a shotgun and show you how to work it after our coffee."

"I thought you'd like to take a bath seeing as how you'll be on a train for three or four days," Sally said.

"We can do both."

"At that same time?"

"That might be difficult."

"Let's do the shotgun first."

Murphy held the shotgun by his side as Sally lit several oil lanterns on the picnic table.

"This is a double-barreled shotgun made by William Moore and Company," Murphy said. "It has a twenty-inch barrel and fires a ten-gauge shell. They call it a coach gun because stagecoach drivers keep one on the seat."

Murphy opened the breech, inserted two shells, and snapped it closed.

"You can fire it from any position," he said and cocked a hammer.

Without aiming, Murphy pulled the trigger and the shotgun blast was so loud Sally thought to cover her ears.

Murphy cocked the hammer and fired the second blast from his hip, turned, and looked at Sally.

"Now you give it a try," Murphy said.

Sally took the weapon from Murphy and

she was surprised at how heavy it was.

"Open the breech and remove the old shells," Murphy said.

Sally opened the breech and removed the spent shells, picked up two from the table, and inserted them into the chambers.

She closed the breech and cocked one hammer.

"Should I aim?" she asked.

"I don't advise that," Murphy said. "Hold it at the hip. There is no need to aim. You will bring down anything within twenty-one feet."

Sally held the shotgun at her hip firmly in two hands and pulled the trigger. It was at that moment that Sally realized just how strong a man Murphy was as the recoil from the shotgun knocked her clean off her feet and onto her duff, and when he fired it he barely moved an inch.

"Maybe we should try something with a bit less bite?" Murphy said.

Sally looked up at Murphy. "That would be good," she said.

Sally watched Murphy change into his trail clothes and the transformation was startling to her. The soft-spoken, almost gentle man seemed to change with each article of clothing he put on into the hardened lawman she met at the railroad camp months ago when he was hunting a killer.

The last item was his gun belt. He slipped it on with a practiced motion and when it was tight and low on his right hip, the transformation was complete.

Murphy the kind, soft-spoken man with a sly sense of humor was gone.

Murphy the regulator had taken his place and Murphy the regulator was the most dangerous man she had ever come across in all of her travels.

Sally slipped on her robe.

"I'll see you out," she said.

Boyle was saddled and ready when they stepped out onto the porch.

The sun was barely up and the sky was caught in twilight.

Murphy kissed Sally on the lips, and then mounted Boyle.

"I'll wire and write whenever I can," Murphy said.

Sally nodded.

Murphy turned Boyle and rode to the road.

Sally watched until he was out of sight and then she entered the house and locked the door.

CHAPTER FOUR

"I can contact the breeder in Maryland where I got my Danes," Burke said. "There should be several litters for sale and Sally can take her pick."

"I appreciate it," Murphy said.

"She didn't strike me as a skittish woman," Burke said.

"Out of her element in a new place," Murphy said. "It makes a woman cautious, especially when alone."

"I understand," Burke said. "I'll ride out and check on her after I see the breeder."

"Appreciate it," Murphy said. "I'll wire you from Denver."

Murphy sat in the chair by the window of his sleeper car and studied the counterfeit bills he took from Burke as samples.

The workmanship was exquisite, the best he'd ever seen. The ten-dollar note was as close to genuine as a forger could make it without the benefit of the presses at the mint and the closely guarded formula for ink. Even the fine hairs on the buffalo looked real.

The twenty-dollar silver certificate was almost as good. The back of the bill with all its intricate design patterns must have been a nightmare to duplicate and must have taken hundreds of hours to carve into printing plates.

Most of the great forgers after the war ended were still serving time in federal prisons. A new crop sprung up in the seventies, but they didn't have the talent or the resources and were quickly shut down.

Murphy took out his small notebook and jotted some notes in pencil.

Wire Burke. Have justice check forgers and counterfeiters released from prison going back five years.

Ask Burke to have a check done of supply houses where ink can be purchased in large quantities and possible sales to private individuals.

Check art houses, print shops, and newspapers for purchases of colored inks.

Check mint and treasury department for retired and terminated engravers and ink mixers in the last five years.

There was a knock on the door and a steward said, "Coffee from room service."

"Door's open," Murphy said.

The steward opened the door and carried a silver tray loaded with coffee pot, creamer, sugar, and spoon into the room and set it on the desk.

"Thank you," Murphy said and gave the steward a dollar in coin.

After the steward left, Murphy filled the cup, splashed in a dollop of milk, and looked out the window as he sipped.

They were somewhere in West Virginia and traveling at fifty miles per hour or more. At this speed, or better, he would arrive in Denver in three and a half days. Only twenty years ago the same journey would have taken months in a covered wagon.

He looked at the notebook.

Tools required to make counterfeit money?

Murphy closed the notebook. He dug out pipe and tobacco pouch, loaded the bowl, and lit up with a wood match.

He took a sip of coffee and sighed softly.

All things considered he'd rather be soaking in a tub full of scented oils with Sally than on a train to Denver.

All things considered.

Sally locked the back door to the house and

all the windows on the first floor. In the kitchen she filled a cup with coffee that was warming on the woodstove and took a seat at the table.

The Winchester rifle Murphy exchanged for the shotgun rested against the side of the table, and she picked it up and set it in front of her. He had shown her how to load the tubular magazine with fifteen rounds, cock the lever, and fire it. The kick wasn't nearly as much as the shotgun and she felt, if the need arose, that she could handle it with some proficiency.

If?

When.

Sally sipped from the cup and stared at the rifle.

Before having lunch in the dining car, Murphy walked back to the last car reserved for horses.

Boyle was the only horse stabled.

As Murphy entered the car, Boyle turned his head and whinnied.

"I'm happy to see you too, boy," Murphy said as he rubbed Boyle's massive neck.

There were brushes and combs on a shelf and Murphy used a brush to smooth out Boyle's mane and back. When his coat shone brightly, Murphy dug out a few sugar

33

cubes he took from the serving tray in his room and hand-fed them to Boyle.

"We're both getting long in the tooth for this kind of work, aren't we, boy?" Murphy said. "I believe after this job we shall retire to Tennessee and sit in the sun with Miss Sally."

Boyle turned his head and looked at Murphy.

"I know what you're thinking, but this time I mean it," Murphy said.

Sally was making a list of items in the kitchen that might be useful to take to Tennessee when she heard a carriage arrive outside.

She picked up the Winchester rifle and went to the window.

It was Burke and he was alone.

Sally went to the door, set the rifle against the wall, unlocked the door, and stepped out to the porch.

"Mr. Burke," she said.

Burke climbed the steps to the porch.

"I hope I haven't come at an inconvenient time," he said.

"No. Just doing odds and ends," Sally said. "Would you like some coffee?"

"I would."

Burke followed Sally into the kitchen,

where she filled two cups at the table.

"Murphy mentioned to me that you would like to get a dog or two," Burke said. "Danes, he said. That's what I have. Two of them."

"I have the feeling that I will spend a great deal of time alone in the house and they make a fine companion and watchdog," Sally said.

"The breeder I purchased mine from is in Maryland, a half day's ride from here," Burke said. "I could wire him and see what he has available and then we can ride out and see if you like any."

"That would be good. Thank you," Sally said.

"Is there anything else I can do for you?" Burke said.

"Not at the moment."

"Then as soon as I hear back from my wire I shall ride out and tell you."

Murphy ate dinner in the dining car at a small table by a window. He dined alone and read a copy of the *Times* and *Post* while he ate.

Before returning to his room he asked for a pot of coffee and carried it with him. He lit three oil lamps, stripped down to underwear, and sat at the desk with his notebook.

He read his notes twice.

He set the notebook aside and reached for his satchel. From it he removed the hundred samples of counterfeit bills in various denominations. He carefully inspected every five-dollar note, then the ten- and finally twenty-dollar notes.

He opened the notebook and picked up a pencil.

All engraving done by one person?

It was impossible to tell the age of the bills by inspection or feel.

They could be a week old or one year. The ink would never entirely dry and the paper disintegrated much quicker than cotton/ linen fibers, especially if wet or left in direct sunlight.

Murphy closed the notebook, finished his coffee, and decided to make it an early night.

Sally hated being afraid.

Before going to bed, she lit the two outside oil lanterns that were mounted on the wall on each side of the door. She lit the interior lanterns on the first floor, four in all, and made sure the doors and windows were locked tight.

In the master bedroom, she placed the Winchester rifle against the chair beside the bed within arm's reach and placed her .32 caliber pistol under Murphy's pillow.

And just because, she kept one lantern on low flame so the room would be slightly illuminated.

The bed was large and cold. After several months of sleeping with Murphy it seemed as if she'd done so all her adult life.

She closed her eyes and waited for morning.

CHAPTER FIVE

Denver was a sprawling city with a population of thirty-five-thousand residents inside the city limits. Add in the metro county and it was closer to fifty thousand.

Citizens rode in carriages or walked. Sidewalks were elevated wood to keep people dry when mud season rolled around. The only men on horseback were visiting cowboys off the trail for a night of fun. Streetlamps were on every corner of every city block. Men were employed to light them at dusk and extinguish them at dawn. Telegraph poles that ran close to the railroad tracks were placed every hundred feet to the station where several poles connected lines to a telegraph office.

The railroad station was almost as large as the station in Washington and certainly the largest in the west.

After retrieving Boyle from his car, Murphy walked him from the station to the center of town where he tethered him to a post outside the Denver Hotel. He removed his Winchester and saddlebags and satchel from the saddle and carried them into the lobby.

Four-stories high, the Denver Hotel was as luxurious as any hotel in Washington, Philadelphia, or New York.

Murphy booked a room for two days with the possibility of a third and paid in advance. He took his satchel, bags, and rifle to his room on the second floor and then returned to Boyle and walked him to the back street where a large livery stable was located.

"As much grain as he wants and give him a good brushing," Murphy told the stable manager.

From the livery to the US Marshal's office was a ten city-block walk. There must have been a recent hard rain because the streets were an inch thick with mud so he stayed on the wood sidewalks except to cross streets.

As he passed several saloons, Murphy noticed the large number of cowboys inside and on the sidewalks. A major cattle stop for cattle drives, one or more must have arrived at the stockyards at the end of town.

At a general store along the way, Murphy

stopped to buy a fresh pouch of tobacco for his pipe. He stuffed the bowl and lit up and continued to the marshal's office.

Murphy spotted Marshal Poule from a block away. Poule was seated in a hardwood chair on the sidewalk in front of his office, rolled cigarette in one hand, tin mug of coffee in the other.

Poule stood up when Murphy reached the office.

"Murphy," Poule said and extended his right hand. "What brings you to Denver?"

Murphy shook Poule's hand. "I'll tell you about it over some coffee. Weren't you in Dodge last time I saw you?"

"We're federal. We get switched around every once in a while to keep us on our toes," Poule said. "Come on, coffee's hot."

Murphy sat in a chair opposite Poule's desk and sipped coffee from a tin mug.

Poule sat behind his desk and studied a few of the counterfeit bills Murphy removed from the flap wallet he stored them in.

"The bank took in several of these just the other day," Poule said. "They took in hundreds of dollars worth last month and sent them to Washington."

"The Bank of Denver?"

"A few shops and stores in town as well,"

Poule said.

"Any idea who passed them?" Murphy said.

"Four major cattle outfits have passed through in the past month," Poule said. "Hundreds of cowboys and they like to get paid in folding money because coin weighs them down. That's four major payrolls shipped in and that doesn't count the miners in town for the silver drilling."

"Let's go talk to the bank," Murphy said.

Walton T. Jacoby was the president of the First Bank of Denver, and as such had the only private office in the building.

From Philadelphia originally, Jacoby came west when the board of the bank he was vice-president of at the time offered him the opportunity to run the largest bank on the frontier. That was twenty years ago and now, nearing sixty years of age, he planned his retirement inside of a year back to Philadelphia as a wealthy man.

"Mr. Jacoby, this is Mr. Murphy from Washington," Poule said when they entered Jacoby's office. "He is with the Secret Service and has some questions for you."

"The Secret Service?" Jacoby said.

"About the counterfeit money you sent to Washington," Murphy said.

41

"Yes, nearly a thousand dollars, in fact," Jacoby said. "We recently took in about two-hundred dollars more."

"May I see the bills?" Murphy said.

Jacoby opened a bottom desk drawer and removed a locked strongbox, opened it with a key, and flipped the lid. From the strong-box Jacoby produced a small stack of bills and set them on the desk.

"Six twenty-dollar notes and seven ten-dollar bills," Jacoby said.

"Can you light the lantern on your desk, please?" Murphy asked.

"It's perfectly daylight," Jacoby said.

Three windows in the office faced the street and the office was well lit from sun-light.

"I know," Murphy said.

Jacoby shrugged and used a wood match to light the oil lantern on the edge of the large desk.

Murphy dug out the flap wallet and re-moved a few twenty-dollar notes and ten-dollar bills. He set them on the desk next to the bills Jacoby produced. From his jacket pocket Murphy took out a magnifying glass and leaned over to study the counterfeit notes.

"How did you detect these bills?" Murphy said.

"Our tellers in the counting room discovered them," Jacoby said. "The ink came off on their hands as if they were still wet."

Murphy looked up from the magnifying glass. "Bundled together in a hot room causes the ink to soften a bit."

Murphy set the magnifying glass on the desk and picked up one of Jacoby's twenty-dollar notes.

"This bill is the work of the same person who made the bills I brought with me," he said.

"How can you tell that?" Jacoby asked.

"The style of design and artwork is exact," Murphy said. "Too exact to be coincidence. The quality of the ink and color is a match. How much money do you have in the bank?"

"About one-hundred thousand in the vault and ten thousand in the tellers' drawers," Jacoby said. "Not counting the payroll money for the two ranchers in town."

"Bank closes at three?" Murphy said.

"Yes, but it's usually four by the time we leave."

"Have your people stay late," Murphy said. "We're going to check every bill."

Jacoby stared at Murphy.

"I wasn't asking," Murphy said.

■ ■ ■ ■

"Do you know where the wagon masters for the two drives are staying in town?" Murphy asked as he and Poule walked along the sidewalk.

"I can tell you both men are registered at the Denver Hotel," Poule said. "Both are probably at the stock pens selling their cattle."

"I need to send a wire," Murphy said.

"Private like last time?"

Murphy nodded.

"While I'm doing that, maybe you can send one of your deputies to contact those cattlemen?" Murphy said.

"Cheevers, this is Mr. Murphy from Washington," Poule said. "He needs to send a telegram."

Cheevers slid a telegram notebook across his desk to Murphy.

"He'll do it himself," Poule said. "You wait outside until he's finished."

"That's against company policy," Cheevers said.

"I won't tell anybody if you won't," Murphy said.

Reluctantly, Cheevers surrendered his

44

desk and went outside with Poule.

Murphy sat at the desk. He placed his finger over the key and began to tap his special identification in Morse code.

Attention Burke Stop White House Stop Need the following information Stop

Murphy tapped in his request. He ended the message with,

No Reply Stop I'll contact you soon Stop Murphy

Murphy sat for a moment, thinking. Then he sent a second telegraph.

Sally Orr Murphy residence Virginia Stop Arrived safe in Denver Stop Will contact you soon Stop Love Murphy

John Chaste and Aaron Burton were lifelong cattlemen. Each had a ranch in Wyoming and twice a year they drove thousands of cattle to Denver for market. Both were tough, sun-baked men with a no-nonsense approach to business.

Both men were with Poule when Murphy returned to the marshal's office.

"John Chaste, Aaron Burton, Mr. Murphy from Washington," Poule said from behind his desk.

"What's this nonsense about fake money?" Chaste said.

"Counterfeit is the word," Murphy said.

"Well, what about it?" Burton said.

"How much money do you have from the drive in profit and payroll?" Murphy asked.

"That's none of your Goddamn business," Chaste said.

Poule looked at Murphy.

Murphy was still for a moment and then softly drew a shallow breath as his face hardened.

"Please don't swear at me again," Murphy said, barely above a whisper.

Chaste stared at Murphy and something in the man's presence reminded him of a coiled rattlesnake.

"Now, I'll ask one more time," Murphy said.

"Forty thousand," Chaste said.

Murphy looked at Burton.

"About the same," Burton said.

"Hotel safe?" Murphy said.

Chaste nodded.

"The marshal will escort you with your cash here later tonight," Murphy said. "We will inspect the bills for counterfeit money."

Chaste and Burton looked at Murphy.

"That's all," Murphy said.

Jacoby, his six tellers, Murphy, and Poule stood before the open safe in the bank vault room.

"Rub each bill for cotton and linen fibers," Murphy said. "The counterfeit bills have a different feel than real money and the ink will run easily with friction."

"This will take hours," Jacoby said.

"Yes it will," Murphy said. "Stack any suspect bills by denominations on the counting table. And maybe somebody could get a couple of pots of coffee?"

Nearly four hours later, Murphy counted three-hundred counterfeit dollars in twenty-dollar notes, two hundred in ten-dollar bills, and one hundred in fives.

"You'll pack and ship the bills to William Burke in Washington," Murphy said. "I'll write down the address."

"Thank God it wasn't more," Jacoby said.

Murphy looked at the tellers.

"Make sure you check every bill coming into the bank and if you get one try to isolate who brought it in, and contact the marshal right away," Murphy said. "It's important to establish an origin."

"We'll count, you watch," Murphy said to Chaste and Burton.

Murphy sat in a chair opposite Poule's desk. Poule sat behind his desk. Each man had a large leather bag that had each rancher's brand etched on the flaps.

Poule opened his bag and dumped stacks of bills on the desk.

"We're going to need more coffee," he said.

"Mr. Burton, your payroll is clean," Murphy said. "Mr. Chaste, we found one-thousand dollars in counterfeit ten- and twenty-dollar bills. The marshal will send the bills to Washington and I'm sorry to say that you're going to have to suffer the loss."

"How does this happen?" Chaste said. "For what reason?"

"It's complicated business, Mr. Chaste," Murphy said. "How much cash did you bring on the trip for payroll and expenses?"

"Five thousand," Chaste said.

"Did you spend it all before you sold your cattle?"

"Just about. A few hundred left in my wallet."

"Let me see the bills."

Chaste dug out his wallet and handed the bills to Murphy.

Murphy inspected the bills and returned them to Chaste.

"They're clean," Murphy said. "So all this money came from auction?"

"Every cent."

"Do you have your receipts?"

"Of course."

Murphy looked at Poule.

"I'll want to talk to the buyers in the morning," he said. "Make sure no one leaves town in the morning."

Poule nodded. "Any idea where all this fake money is coming from?"

"No. Want to talk about it over a steak?"

"I have to admit I know next to nothing about the buying and selling of the cattle business," Murphy said. "Denver is a major stop because of the railroad, but it's mostly cash and carry isn't it?"

The hotel dining room stayed open until midnight and they served an excellent steak with trimmings.

"In the old days before the railroad, ranchers would have to drive their herds hundreds of miles to main outlets like Omaha. A drive could take months," Poule said. "Now they can drive their herds to Denver, sell them to different beef houses, and the railroad ships them off to Omaha and as far east as Chicago."

"The buyers travel with large sums of money?" Murphy asked.

"And bodyguards armed to the teeth," Poule said.

"Where do they keep their cash?"

"The auction house office in a safe under armed guards."

"The cattle being shipped out tomorrow?"

"The railroad has scheduled extra trains to take cattle east, I think starting at ten."

"Let's have breakfast at seven-thirty so we have time to talk to the buyers," Murphy said.

Alone in his hotel room, Murphy dug out the bottle of his father's whiskey from his satchel, filled his pipe with fresh tobacco, and sat at the desk to write Sally a letter.

He was surprised that he wrote more than two pages.

He ended with, *No need to reply because I'll be on the move. Know that I miss and love you. Murphy.*

CHAPTER SIX

R.J. Pickering bought and sold cattle for various slaughterhouses back east and on the frontier for thirty years. A large man with a round stomach, he stared at Murphy as Marshal Poule told him why he had been escorted to Poule's office by a deputy.

"What are you accusing me of?" Pickering said.

"Nothing," Poule said.

"Then why the hell did you drag me away from my business?" Pickering said. "I have a train to catch."

"What part of counterfeit money didn't you understand?" Murphy said.

Pickering looked carefully at Murphy, at the man's height and the way he wore his gun, and he didn't like what he saw.

"And who the hell are you?" Pickering said.

"Murphy."

"Well, you got the marshal kissing your

ass so you must be somebody important," Pickering said. "What do you want?"

"You purchased five-hundred head of cattle from Mr. Chaste," Murphy said.

"What of it?"

"You paid him in cash," Murphy said. "One-thousand dollars of it was in counterfeit money."

Pickering looked at Poule and the marshal didn't move a muscle.

"It's not my money," Pickering said. "The money belongs to the companies I'm hired to buy for."

"I know that," Murphy said. "What companies did you buy for?"

"Dodge Cattle and Omaha Beef," Pickering said.

"You got the money how?" Murphy asked.

"Bank draft out of Dodge City First National."

"Who runs Dodge Cattle?" Murphy said.

"M.K. Ritchie," Pickering said. "Although I've never met the man. He recently acquired the company from an outfit in Chicago."

"And Omaha Beef?"

"A board of directors, that's all I know."

"Thank you for your time, Mr. Pickering," Murphy said.

"That's it?" Pickering asked.

"That's it, Mr. Pickering, unless you've been withholding information from me," Murphy said.

After Pickering left the office, Murphy stuffed his pipe, lit it with a match, and said, "I believe I'll walk over to the depot and check train schedules to Dodge City."

"Who is the new marshal in Dodge?" Murphy asked.

"That would be Jack Adams," Poule said. "He's a good man. Worked Dodge back in the old days. Spent some time north and took over again when I left."

"Wire him I should be arriving around midnight tonight," Murphy said. "If he could hold a room for me at any hotel that would be good."

"If the bank finds anymore counterfeit money?" Poule asked.

"Send it along to Washington."

Murphy and Poule shook hands.

"Safe trip," Poule said.

Murphy boarded the train at the riding car and entered.

The ride to the breeder's kennel took just over four hours in Burke's carriage. Gratefully, Burke drove and they were alone on the trip. The countryside was gorgeous with forests of white birch trees along the way.

The breeder had a large facility on forty acres of land. There were forty individual kennels and several types of dog breeds were on display. Besides Danes, he bred Boxers, German Shepherds, retrievers, and pinchers.

Danes, Boxers, and Shepherds were used mostly for protection, the breeder explained, while the retrievers and pinchers were retrieving dogs used mostly by duck and bird hunters.

Sally selected a ten-week-old pair of Dane puppies from the same litter that would be ready to take home in two weeks.

"The males make better watchdogs than the females," the breeder said. "Especially for a woman. They become very protective and will attack an intruder on sight. They will guard a child with their life."

They were exactly what Sally wanted. She paid for the dogs and then she and Burke made the return trip to Virginia.

Murphy ate lunch in the dining car and then took a nap in a riding car by the window.

He awoke with seven hours travel time remaining and he carried his satchel to the dining car and ordered a pot of coffee. He pulled out the notebook and studied his notes, then dug out a pencil.

Counterfeiter needs an outlet for the money. Small amounts scattered about are a test run to see if bills will pass inspection at banks and stores. They do.

What price on the dollar for American counterfeit money?

"A good question," Murphy said aloud, and sipped some coffee.

After Burke dropped Sally off at Murphy's home, at her insistence, he waited for her to go inside and then wave from the window before he drove to the road and back to Washington.

Night was falling, but Burke knew the way back well enough that traveling in the dark was not a problem, especially if he lit the two oil lanterns mounted on the front of the carriage where the horses wouldn't see them.

Strange that Sally seemed so skittish now that Murphy was in Denver. Burke knew what Sally was back in Saint Louis and for the railroads, but that was behind her now, and besides, a woman needed to be tough to run a large brothel.

He thought of asking her, but decided against it. If the problem was serious enough she probably would have mentioned it during the ride to the breeder.

Hopefully the information Murphy wanted would be on his desk when he dropped off the carriage and did a quick check of his mail.

Arthur was proving to be less patient than Garfield and Burke didn't want to upset the presidential apple cart.

Or Murphy's for that matter.

If it came down to who would win an argument between the president and Murphy, Burke's money was on the regulator.

The train arrived in Dodge City a few minutes past midnight. The stop on the express train to Chicago was unscheduled, but because of Murphy's government status, the railroad agreed to make the stop in Dodge.

US Marshal Jack Adams and two deputies were waiting on the platform for Murphy when he retrieved Boyle and walked to them.

"Mr. Murphy?" Adams asked.

"Yes. Marshal Jack Adams?" Murphy said.

"You must carry a lot of sway with the railroad to make an unscheduled stop, Mr.

Murphy," Adams said.

"I'll tell you about it over a drink," Murphy said. "As soon as I stable my horse."

The Dodge House Saloon and Gambling Emporium had forty tables for drinking, six tables for card games, the like number in roulette wheels, a thirty-foot-long bar, plenty of saloon girls, and a first-rate piano player. It was by far the largest and most prestigious drinking establishment in town.

Although closing time was one in the morning, nearly every table was occupied, as was the bar.

Murphy and Adams shared a small table by the large picture window.

"I haven't been to Dodge in quite a while," Murphy said.

"Nothing's changed," Adams said. "It's still a cowboy town except that half the cows arrive by railroad now."

Murphy sipped his shot of bourbon and glanced around the room.

"Busy night," he said.

"A hundred or more cowboys in town and every last one of them is itching to spend three months' pay," Adams said.

"This place does well," Murphy said.

"Closes at one, but whoever is still inside when they lock the doors can stay until two," Adams said. "But, you didn't travel from Denver on a special stop to talk about a saloon."

"No. Counterfeit money has been passed in several states and territories in the west recently," Murphy said. "Usually the workmanship is so poor it's spotted right away, but this is different. The work is close to flawless and has fooled even banks."

"Kansas?"

"Yes. Do you know a man named Pickering?"

"Cattle broker, sure. Known him for years. Whenever drive time rolls around Pickering is always front and center. He has a keen eye for cattle and knows how to buy."

"He bought cattle in Denver for the Dodge Cattle Company for M.K. Ritchie and some of the money he used was counterfeit," Murphy said. "The money came from the Dodge City First National Bank."

"How much money?" Adams asked.

"One thousand dollars in tens and twenties."

"I don't know much about counterfeit money, but for a thousand dollars to slip under a bank's nose it would have to be good," Adams said.

"Tomorrow morning I'd like to speak with the bank president and Mr. Ritchie," Murphy said.

Adams took a sip of his drink and then grinned.

"What?" Murphy said.

"You can speak with the bank president for sure, but seeing Mr. Ritchie might be a problem," Adams said.

"Why?"

"M.K. Ritchie is Mary Kate Ritchie, that's why."

"A woman owns the Dodge Cattle Company?" Murphy asked, a bit surprised.

"Jepson Ritchie founded the company back in fifty-one when there was nothing out here except trails heading west and Indians," Adams said. "Mary Kate, his only child as his wife died in delivery, was raised on the cattle business. Jepson died in seventy-three and she took control of the company. You'd be hard pressed to find anybody who knows more about the cattle business than her."

"I'm not here for the cattle business," Murphy said. "I'm interested in the counterfeit money she sent Pickering to Denver with to buy cattle."

"She does a lot of business with the bank here in town, but with other banks back east, too," Adams said.

"I figured," Murphy said. "But I have to

start a paper trail somewhere."

"Exactly how good is this fake money?" Adams asked.

"Got any folding money on you?" Murphy said.

Adams reached into a pocket on his vest and dug out some folded bills, one of which was a twenty.

"Set that twenty on the table," Murphy said.

Adams unfolded the twenty-dollar note and placed it on the table as Murphy dug out a counterfeit twenty and placed it so the two bills were side-by-side.

Adams stared at the two notes.

"Shit," Adams said.

"About what the president said, I imagine," Murphy said.

Adams picked up both bills and inspected them carefully.

"Impossible to tell," he said.

"I'll see the bank first and then Miss Ritchie," Murphy said. "Is there a good place for breakfast we can meet around eight?"

"The Dodge Café is as good as any," Adams said.

"See you at eight," Murphy said.

Sally opened her eyes when a loud noise

from outside woke her.

She stayed motionless in bed and listened until she heard the noise a second time. Then she got up, tossed on her robe, and grabbed the Winchester rifle.

She left the room and as quietly as possible walked down the stairs. She hated the feeling of fear, of being afraid of noises in the dark, but she hated the fear of not knowing the source even more.

At the front door, she cocked the lever of the Winchester, then unlocked and slowly opened the door.

The lanterns illuminated the porch fairly well and the full moon cast enough light on the ground to see a good forty feet in every direction.

She stepped outside.

At the far end of the porch two raccoons stared at her.

Sally sighed openly with relief.

"Go on you two, get," she said.

The raccoons scattered off the porch. Sally watched them wander into the dark woods and then went inside and locked the door.

CHAPTER SEVEN

Thomas Mason had the thickest Yankee accent Murphy had ever come across this side of the North End in Boston. He not only sounded like an eastern dude, he dressed the part, wearing a fancy banker-type suit you'd expect to see in Boston and New York.

Sent by the parent company of the Dodge Bank in Boston, Mason was in his third year as bank president. It struck Murphy that Mason had done well for a man still in his mid-thirties.

Behind his desk, Mason inspected the ten- and twenty-dollar bills Murphy set down and said, "Excellent workmanship, but I can assure you they didn't pass through my tellers."

Murphy had to strain to understand the thick accent. "How can you be sure of that?" Murphy asked.

"I train all tellers and employees of the bank personally," Mason said. "These bills are of the highest quality, but I assure you they wouldn't pass inspection."

"They should, those bills are real," Murphy said.

Behind Murphy, Marshal Adams stifled a laugh.

"What did you say?" Mason said.

"That ten and twenty are real," Murphy said.

Mason looked at the two bills and then glared at Murphy. "What kind of stunt are you trying to pull here, Murphy?"

"No stunt," Murphy said. "Just making the point that anybody could be fooled."

"Well, you made your point at my expense," Mason said. "Is there anything else I can do for you besides playing the fool? I'm a busy man."

"At closing time today you'll have a complete audit done of every bill in your safe and teller drawers," Murphy said.

"That would take hours," Mason said.

"It would," Murphy said.

"Mr. Murphy, did you come here just to make me appear an idiot?" Mason said.

"You're doing a good job of that on your own," Murphy said. "Now, either you have a complete audit done after closing today or I will have six Secret Service agents in town in three days and they will close your bank for one week and do the audit for you. Which?"

"Can he do that?" Mason said to Adams.

"Oh, yes," Adams said.

"Today good enough?" Mason asked.

"Yes," Murphy said. "About the Dodge Cattle Company, does Miss Ritchie have an account with you?"

"For regular business," Mason said. "For a major drive, Wells Fargo delivers a sealed box to the bank and I lock it in our safe."

"Uncounted?"

"It arrives sealed and it gets delivered to her sealed."

"Thank you for your time," Murphy said. "I'll be back later to help with the audit."

"I can hardly wait," Mason said.

The Dodge Cattle Company occupied a stand-alone, two-story building across the street from the stock-holding pens.

The first floor of the building had a massive plate-glass window with the words **Dodge Cattle Company M.K. Ritchie** etched across the bottom. Even from across the street Murphy could see four desks with one man seated at each desk.

A telegraph pole stood next to the building with two lines, one for the first floor and the other for the second floor.

On the left side of the building a wood staircase led to the second-floor office of Mary Kate Ritchie.

Murphy smoked his pipe as he leaned against a fence of a holding pen. Beside him, Marshal Adams rolled a paper cigarette.

"I don't pretend to understand it, but the line to the first floor is hooked up to an electrified ticker-tape machine that gives stock reports from New York as they happen," Adams said. "I've been in there a few times when little scrolls of paper roll out and they send and receive telegrams and buy and sell commodities and stocks. They seem to get real excited about it."

"Who else works with Miss Ritchie?" Murphy asked.

"There is Mr. Ren Norio Kyoto from Japan," Adams said. "He's been sent from his government to study the American cattle business to upgrade the way they do things back home, I guess. He's been in town three days."

"What time did you say she'd see us?" Murphy asked.

"Eleven."

Murphy pulled out his pocket watch.

"That would be now," he said.

Murphy and Adams crossed the street and

climbed the stairs to the second floor. A brass plate with the name M.K. Ritchie was mounted on the wood door.

Murphy knocked.

The door was opened by a Japanese man a foot shorter than Murphy.

"Miss Ritchie?" Murphy said.

The man opened the door and stepped out of the way.

Mary Kate Ritchie sat behind a large oak desk. Seated opposite her, Ren Norio Kyoto looked at Murphy and stood up. Besides the short man who answered the door, two other Japanese men stood in the room off to one side.

Mary Kate stood up. She was a tall woman of five-foot seven inches or so, with black shoulder-length hair and piercing black eyes. She wore riding pants and a denim shirt and boots.

Kyoto stood an inch or so shorter than Mary Kate. He was a slight man with a pencil-thin mustache and jet-black hair parted on the left side. His suit was hand-made of fine linen.

The two men on the side were taller, stouter, wore less expensive suits, and had long, black ponytails.

"Hello, Marshal," Mary Kate said.

"Morning," Adams said. "This is Mr.

Murphy from Washington. The man I told you about."

"This is Mr. Ren Norio Kyoto from Japan," Mary Kate said. "He's here to study the ways of the American cattle business."

Murphy looked at Kyoto.

"How do you do, Mr. Murphy," Kyoto said.

"You speak English very well," Murphy said.

"I was taught as a child in Japan and then sent to business school in London," Kyoto said. "I lived there for four years."

"Mr. Kyoto is spending two weeks with me and he has learned almost as much as it took me thirty years to learn," Mary Kate said.

"You are too modest, Miss Ritchie," Kyoto said.

"Ren, I have to see Mr. Murphy about some government business," Mary Kate said. "Can we pick this up after lunch?"

"Of course."

Kyoto seemed to bow at Murphy without moving. He waited for the two bodyguards and a smaller, third man to exit first and then he followed them out of the office.

Mary Kate took her chair and looked up at Murphy.

"My time is valuable," she said.

"But your counterfeit money is not," Murphy said.

Mary Kate looked at Adams for a moment, then shifted her eyes back to Murphy.

"My counterfeit money?" she said.

"You gave Pickering cash to buy cattle for your company," Murphy said. "One thousand of it was counterfeit. That makes it yours."

"Mine in the sense that I sent for the money from the Bank of Wells Fargo," Mary Kate said.

"How much all told?"

"Forty thousand."

"Did you count it?"

"My people did."

"They missed it," Murphy said. "Maybe you should count it yourself next time."

"I would say, Mr. Murphy, that Wells Fargo missed it," Mary Kate said. She smiled. "Wouldn't you?"

"Marshal Adams, did you know I can arrest someone for the federal crime of trafficking in counterfeit money?" Murphy said.

Mary Kate's smile vanished.

"And all I need is suspicion," Murphy said.

Mary Kate's eyes narrowed to hard slits. "Suspicion of what?" she said.

"Deliberately passing counterfeit money."

"That's a lie."

"No, it's a fact," Murphy said. "Just like lying to a federal officer is a crime. Marshal, would you escort Miss Ritchie over to your office and stick her in a cell?" Murphy said. "I'll wire Washington and have a Secret Service train come pick her up in three days."

"Three days in a . . . ," Mary Kate said. "Murphy, you are no gentleman. However, as I do not cherish the idea of sitting in the marshal's filthy cell for three days I shall make a slight confession to you."

"Make it a full confession," Murphy said.

"The money arrived from Wells Fargo as usual on the train with an armed escort," Mary Kate said. "I took possession of it with the marshal and two of his deputies and we walked it over to my office downstairs where it was locked up in my safe until three days ago when Mr. Pickering took possession of it."

"When was it counted?" Murphy said.

"The day it arrived."

"Who counted it?"

"My men downstairs."

"Where were you?"

"Right here with Mr. Kyoto and his people."

"And your men discovered one-thousand dollars was counterfeit?"

"Yes. They are well trained and have been with me for years."

"And then?"

"I told them to pack it as is and give it to Mr. Pickering."

"Why not wire Wells Fargo and have them replace the thousand?"

"Normally I would have, but there wasn't time," Mary Kate said. "And besides, I fuc . . . screwed up when I signed for the money before it was counted. I'll never make that mistake again. It was the first time in eleven years of doing business with Wells Fargo Bank that this has happened."

"So you figured they wouldn't have discovered the counterfeit bills in Denver?" Murphy said.

"Did they?"

"No."

"Then I figured right."

"Where was the money shipped from?"

"Philadelphia."

Murphy nodded.

"I'd like to see your safe."

"It's empty at the moment."

"Miss Ritchie, I wasn't asking," Murphy said.

Mary Kate stared at Murphy.

She stood up and walked out from behind the desk to the door. Murphy and Adams followed her down the stairs. She walked with a noticeable sway to her hips as the riding pants hugged her like skin.

In the office, the four men froze at their desks.

A ticker-tape machine tapped lightly in the background, spewing out a thin trail of paper to the floor.

"Relax, boys," Mary Kate said. "Mr. Murphy wants to examine our safe."

Murphy noted immediately that the safe was a Mosler safe, probably an 1875 model that weighed three-thousand pounds.

"I bought this safe a year after my father died," Mary Kate said. "I felt the 1867 model wasn't secure enough."

"Open it," Murphy said.

"Why?"

"Because I asked you to," Murphy said.

Mary Kate stood before the safe to shield the tumbler lock with her body and spun the dial to the four digits required to unlock the safe. On the fourth spin there was a click and she pulled the heavy door open.

"Close it and lock it and open it again," Murphy said.

Mary Kate glared at Murphy, but she closed the safe door and spun the dial. She was about to move the dial to the first number when Murphy knelt beside the safe and looked at Adams.

"Hand me that empty water glass there on the desk," Murphy said.

Adams picked up the glass and gave it to Murphy.

Murphy placed the opening of the glass against the side of the safe and pressed his right ear to the bottom of the glass.

"Go ahead, open it," he said.

Mary Kate slowly spun the dial left and right, stopping four times, and then moved the arm down and pulled open the safe.

Murphy stood and set the water glass on the desk.

"Do you have a doctor in town?" he asked.

"Two," Adams said.

Murphy looked at the four men at their desks.

"One of you men fetch a doctor and ask him to bring his bag," Murphy said.

One of the men stood up and left the office.

Murphy dug his pipe out of his pocket and a bag of tobacco. He filled the bowl, struck a match, and looked at Mary Kate.

"How much did that safe cost?"

"Six-hundred dollars. Why?"

Murphy looked at Adams.

"Is there a skilled gunsmith in town?" he asked.

"The Swede," Adams said.

"Mr. Murphy, what is . . . ?" Mary Kate said.

"I'll answer your questions when the doctor gets here," Murphy said.

"Who is ill?" Mary Kate said.

Murphy looked at the three men at their desks. "One of you men fetch the gunsmith. Tell him Miss Ritchie needs his services."

"Everybody stay put. Mr. Murphy, I don't see how any of this is your business," Mary Kate said. "Or has to do with the counterfeit money."

The door opened and the doctor and Mary Kate's employee walked in. A small man of about sixty, the doctor held his black bag in his right hand and looked at Mary Kate.

"Who is ill?" the doctor asked.

"Nobody, but I am in need of your stethoscope," Murphy said.

"My . . . who are you?" the doctor asked.

"Doc, let him borrow the stethoscope," Adams said.

The doctor set his bag on a desk, opened it, and removed the stethoscope and handed it to Murphy.

Murphy looked at the man who brought

the doctor.

"Can you tell the gunsmith Miss Ritchie is in need of his services here in the office?" Murphy said.

The man nodded and left the office again.

Murphy put the earpieces in his ears, knelt before the safe, and placed the listening tube over the tumbler on the safe.

Slowly turning the dial left, right, and left again, Murphy stopped the dial four times before he stood up and removed the earpieces. He grabbed the arm handle, pushed it down, and pulled open the safe door.

"I would have never believed opening a safe could be so easy," Adams said.

Murphy looked at Mary Kate.

She met him with a cold stare.

"When you lock up at night what is your procedure?" Murphy asked.

"The men lock the door with two interior deadbolts and one drop bar," Mary Kate said. "They set the electric bell alarm over there on the desk that is wired to the telegraph. If someone breaks in through the door or glass window the alarm bell rings. It's the latest in alarms from back east."

Murphy walked to the closed door and inspected the wired contacts on the door and window. They were intact.

He turned and looked at Mary Kate.

"So they lock up from the inside, how do they leave?"

"This way," Mary Kate said.

Murphy and Adams followed Mary Kate into a narrow hallway off the main office where she opened a door. She went up the stairs with them behind her and opened a door and stepped into the back room of her office.

"They lock this door and go to my door and lock it with a key," she said, stepping into her office.

Murphy looked at the door and quickly scanned the office.

"I suggest you install a bell alarm on this door as well," he said.

The door on the first floor opened and closed and Adams said, "That must be the Swede."

The Swede had no accent at all, and in fact wasn't even Swedish. He was called the Swede simply because he had blond hair as did most Swedish immigrants in the area.

"Oil the interior components of Miss Ritchie's safe and then install a key-lock system that backs up the tumbler lock," Murphy told the Swede. "Even if you know the combination the safe won't open without the key. Can you do that?"

After a quick inspection of the safe, the

Swede nodded. "Cost ya," he said.

"Do it," Mary Kate said.

Murphy looked at Mary Kate.

"Good afternoon," he said.

"How long will you be in town Mr. Murphy?" Mary Kate said.

"Not sure. A few more days at least."

"Maybe we'll see each other again."

"Maybe."

"I need to send a telegram," Murphy said as he and Adams walked back to the center of town.

"Western Union is right up the street from my office," Adams said.

"What do you mean wait outside?" the telegraph operator said.

"It's a private conversation," Murphy said.

The operator looked at Adams.

Adams nodded.

The operator and Adams went outside and stood on the wood sidewalk.

Murphy sat at the desk and tapped in his private code to the White House.

Attention William Burke Stop Send requested information to Dodge City to US Marshal Adams Stop No reply Stop Murphy

Murphy stepped outside.

"Let's get a steak and then I'll give the banker a hand with the audit," Murphy said to Adams.

CHAPTER EIGHT

Sally came back from a walk in the fields to find a letter on the porch balanced against the door. She had taken the Winchester rifle with her and she set one down and picked up the other.

The letter was from Murphy.

She sat on a chair and tore the envelope open and removed the three folded pages.

Murphy started the letter by telling her he missed and loved her. Then he detailed his exploits of the trip west and what he was working on. He asked about the dogs and the packing for the move and ended the letter by telling her he missed and loved her again and would try to get back home as soon as possible.

Sally folded the letter back into the envelope.

She felt something wet on her face and realized that she had been crying.

Murphy was seated on a chair on the porch of the Dodge Hotel with a cup of coffee, his pipe, and writing paper. He was halfway through a letter to Sally when Mary Kate Ritchie arrived in a carriage driven by herself.

"Mr. Murphy, good morning," she said.

"Morning," Murphy said.

"I'm taking Mr. Kyoto to see my ranch outside of town," Mary Kate said. "Would you like to come along? Mr. Kyoto is an interesting man to talk to."

"I'll saddle my horse," Murphy said, as he tucked the letter into his jacket pocket.

"No need if you ride up here with me," Mary Kate said.

"All right."

Murphy stepped off the porch and into the carriage beside Mary Kate.

"Mr. Kyoto is waiting at my office," Mary Kate said and handed the reins to Murphy.

"I suppose I owe you a thank you for what you did in my office," Mary Kate said.

"No need."

Behind them Kyoto and his three men followed in a large carriage. The small man who answered the door to Murphy held the reins.

"How did the audit at the bank go?" Mary

79

Kate said.

"Odd, but the only counterfeit money we found were in two cashier tills. Each a twenty-dollar note," Murphy said.

"That means someone passed it to the bank yesterday," Mary Kate said. "Somebody in town."

"There are a hundred or more cowboys in town," Murphy said. "All paid in cash. Cowboys like to exchange large bills for smaller ones because they think they'll drink less in a saloon if they're carrying small bills."

"And do they?"

"No."

Mary Kate smiled.

"I suppose you're wondering why I'm thirty-two years old and not married," she said.

"Nope."

"Would you like to know why?"

"Nope."

"You're quite the conversationalist."

"Your father was in on the ground floor of the cattle business and after your mother died he raised you to be a cattle woman," Murphy said. "You learned at his knee and after he died you took over a medium-size business and turned it into a large eight-million head of cattle business. Now you want to turn your large company into an empire. You can't do that saddled with a husband and a house full of kids. Is that about it?"

Mary Kate looked at Murphy.

"I am trying very hard to like you, Mr. Murphy," she said. "You are making that rather difficult."

"How much longer to your ranch?" Murphy said.

"About an hour."

"You don't make this trip every day?"

"No. I have a house in town. I live there. My foreman runs the ranch."

"Tell me about Mr. Kyoto."

"I can only tell you what I know of the man from the past week or so."

"That will do."

"He's a Japanese diplomat as you know," Mary Kate said. "His government has sent him to America to study our cattle business so he can help Japan grow their own cattle industry using modern, western techniques. He is a gentleman as you witnessed and very smart and educated. The small man with him is his manservant. The other two are his bodyguards. In Japan they were samurai warriors. Do you know what that is?"

"Yes."

"I didn't. See the road coming up on the

81

left? Turn there."

The sign above the archway entrance to Mary Kate's ranch read, **Dodge City Cattle Company. Jepson Ritchie Founder. M.K. Ritchie President.**

From the archway to the main house was just over a half mile.

On both sides of the dirt road to the house were fences that seemed to stretch as far as the eye could see.

"If you're wondering why there are no cattle in the fences, I shipped five-thousand head to Omaha, Texas, and Chicago," Mary Kate said. "We have two-thousand on the ranges and when the shipment from Denver arrives another five-hundred."

"Breeding?" Murphy asked.

"That's correct."

They arrived at the large ranch-style house and Murphy parked the carriage by the gate. Kyoto's carriage parked directly behind it. Murphy stepped down and took Mary Kate's hand and helped her to the ground.

She was wearing riding clothes, as was Kyoto and his two bodyguards.

"Mr. Kyoto, are you ready to do some riding?" Mary Kate said.

Kyoto bowed slightly. "Very much so," he said.

A lean cowboy wearing chaps came out of the barn to the side of the house and walked to Mary Kate.

"Horses are saddled and ready to go," he said.

"This is Mr. Lomax, my ranch foreman," Mary Kate said.

Kyoto bowed slightly.

"We will need an extra horse for Mr. Murphy," Mary Kate said.

Lomax looked at Murphy.

"Can you handle a large male?" he said.

Murphy nodded. "Mind if I saddle him?"

Ten minutes later, with all but Kyoto's manservant atop a horse, Mary Kate said, "Take us to the south range, Mr. Lomax."

Lomax rode point, with Murphy, Mary Kate, and Kyoto behind him and Kyoto's two bodyguards behind them.

"You ride well, Mr. Kyoto, but try to lean back slightly and let the horse do the work," Mary Kate said. "It will save wear on your back. Look at Mr. Murphy, at how he rides."

Kyoto turned and looked at Murphy. In the saddle, Murphy sat slightly aback and appeared completely at ease with the horse.

Kyoto nodded, smiled, and did his best to

imitate Murphy.

At the south range, cowboys roped and branded dozens of young cattle with the Dodge Cattle Company brand.

"My men are branding strays missed during the spring roundup," Mary Kate told Kyoto.

"I understand," Kyoto said.

"You see, Mr. Kyoto, I not only buy cattle at prime interest rates for market, I also raise my own," Mary Kate said. "If you want to know why, it's to protect my interest against a bad year or years where ranchers don't have enough cattle to bring to market. There was a drought in seventy-six that nearly wiped out hundreds of thousands of cattle across five states. I have water and enough grazing land to support ten times what I could buy. Understand?"

"Very much so," Kyoto said.

"Do your bodyguards rope?" Mary Kate said.

"They are excellent riders, but they are not cowboys," Kyoto said.

"Don't they brand the cattle in your country?" Mary Kate said.

"Yes."

"Riding and roping are a big part of the business," Mary Kate said. "Maybe they could learn and when you return home they could teach others."

"Yes, I agree," Kyoto said.

"Mr. Lomax, would you and the men instruct Mr. Kyoto's men on how to rope and brand," Mary Kate said.

"Do they speak English?" Lomax asked.

"They do when I allow it," Kyoto said.

Kyoto looked at his bodyguards and instructed them to go with Lomax and to speak English to him.

Both bodyguards bowed and followed Lomax.

"Mr. Kyoto, while they are doing that please walk with me a bit," Mary Kate said. "You, too, Mr. Murphy."

Kyoto and Murphy walked beside Mary Kate about a thousand feet to a small open range next to a sloping hill of grasslands.

Several dozen head or so of Texas Longhorn cattle grazed on tall sweet grass.

"Have you ever seen cattle such as these, Mr. Kyoto?" Mary Kate asked.

"I have not."

"They are called Texas Longhorns," Mary Kate said. "And as you can see from their yard-long horns, they live up to their name."

"They are exquisite," Kyoto said.

"I am going to make a gift of two males and two females to you, Mr. Kyoto," Mary

Kate said. "I will arrange to have them shipped to Japan in your name as a gift to your emperor."

Kyoto bowed graciously to Mary Kate.

"I am humbled by your generosity," he said.

"Think nothing of it," Mary Kate said. "Let's check on your bodyguards."

They returned to the range where one of Kyoto's bodyguards was on a horse and doing his best to rope a young steer and failing miserably.

"It is not as easy as your men make it appear," Kyoto said.

"No, it isn't," Mary Kate said. "Mr. Murphy, have you ever roped a steer?"

"I'm a fair hand with a rope, but I haven't roped a steer since I left the Army," Murphy said.

"Care to try?" Mary Kate asked.

"Not my line of work," Murphy said.

"No, I suppose not," Mary Kate said.

She turned to Kyoto.

"Mr. Kyoto, would you care for some lunch?" Mary Kate said. "My cook is an excellent chef."

The dining room in the ranch house had a table large enough to hold twenty, but just Mary Kate, Kyoto, and Murphy were there for lunch.

"I asked the cook to try some different spices that might remind you of home, Mr. Kyoto," Mary Kate said. "Do you approve?"

Lunch was grilled steak flavored with several types of spices, white rice, and green beans with peapods.

"Very much so," Kyoto said. "Where did he obtain them?"

"I picked them up at the general store in town and had them sent to the ranch."

"They are excellent."

"Mr. Murphy?"

"I agree, excellent."

"Mr. Murphy, you are a policeman?" Kyoto said.

"In a sense," Murphy said. "I work for the federal government."

"Then you are aware that your government sent a large contingent of soldiers from your Army to Japan to teach us modern warfare in eighteen seventy-five," Kyoto said.

"I'm aware," Murphy said.

"We learned much, but we lost much as well," Kyoto said. "We wear western clothes like Americans and the samurai, after a thousand years of service, are no more. Modern armies with modern weapons now protect the emperor. I fear the next century will change Japan forever."

"Do you know who Charles Darwin is?" Murphy said.

"I have read a bit about him and his theories," Kyoto said.

"Then you know he discovered flightless birds on the Galapagos Islands," Murphy said. "Because they have nowhere to fly to, these birds have lost the ability to fly."

Kyoto nodded at Murphy.

"I understand your meaning and you make much sense," he said.

"I don't," Mary Kate said.

"Mr. Murphy is saying that if Japan doesn't adapt along with the modern world it will become like that flightless bird and get left behind," Kyoto said.

"Mr. Murphy is far more educated than he lets on," Mary Kate said.

"He is also correct," Kyoto said. "The samurai, as well trained in archery and with swords, are no match for repeating rifles and military explosives. Your sidearm, Mr. Murphy, that is not the sidearm your Army had when they came to my country."

"This is a Colt Peacemaker chambered in .44 ammunition, the same as my Winchester rifle," Murphy said. "I can travel without having to carry two kinds of ammunition. The Army probably wore Smith&Wesson

Schofield sidearms and I often use that myself when called for."

"Tell us, Mr. Murphy, what other parlor tricks do you have up your sleeve?" Mary Kate said. "I've seen you open my safe without knowing the combination, what other little tricks are you master of?"

Murphy looked at Mary Kate.

"Have you a pencil?" he said.

"A pencil?"

"And a sheet of writing paper."

Mary Kate stood up and left the dining room. She returned a minute later with a long pencil and a stack of writing paper.

"Mr. Kyoto, have you a pocket knife?" Murphy asked.

Kyoto reached into a jacket pocket and set a small jackknife on the table.

Murphy removed two sheets of paper and set them next to each other.

"Mr. Kyoto, on the paper closest to you, press your thumb on it and hold it down for a moment."

Kyoto pressed his thumb on the paper for a count of three.

"Good," Murphy said.

He picked up Kyoto's jackknife, opened the blade, and started to whittle the wood casing away on the pencil over the paper closest to him. When the wood had been removed, Murphy held the exposed stick of graphite over the sheet of paper Kyoto pressed his thumb on and whittled the graphite to a fine powder.

"That should do," Murphy said.

He set the jackknife down and picked up the paper and gently rocked it back and forth to spread the graphite powder, then just as gently held the paper over the other sheet and softly blew the powder off, exposing Kyoto's thumbprint.

"Every person on the planet has a set of fingerprints and no two are alike," Murphy said. "Like snowflakes."

Kyoto stared at his thumbprint, and then looked at his thumb.

"Everything you touch that has a smooth surface will have your prints on it," Murphy said. "They follow you around like your shadow."

Delighted, Kyoto smiled and bowed his head slightly to Murphy.

"Most impressive, Mr. Murphy," Kyoto said.

"Well, if you're through bedazzling us, Mr. Murphy, how about some coffee on the porch?" Mary Kate said.

Burke took a sip of coffee, nodded his approval, and said, "My reason for stopping by is that I am sending Murphy a package by express railroad tonight and I thought you might like to add a note to it."

"I would," Sally said. "That's very thoughtful of you. Where is he at the moment?"

"Dodge City."

"For how long?"

"At least until he receives the package. Two, maybe three days. I'm not sure."

"Have some more coffee while I go inside and write a note."

Burke rose as Sally stood up from her chair and entered the house. He looked at Christopher, who sat in the driver's seat of his carriage.

"Why not have some of this coffee while we wait?" Burke said.

Christopher, grinning, hopped off the seat and climbed the steps to the porch.

"Believe I will," Christopher said.

The sky was darkening when Murphy stopped the carriage in front of the two-story, gray and yellow house at the end of Elm Street about a mile from Mary Kate's office.

A white picket fence surrounded the home and a lush garden full of flowers lined both sides of a walkway to the door.

"Big place for one person," Murphy said as he stepped down.

Mary Kate took Murphy's hand and she stepped down next to him.

"My cook and housekeeper live with me," she said.

"Where do you keep your carriage?"

"My cook will drive it over to the livery."

"It's a short walk to my hotel," Murphy said. "I'll say goodnight."

"Goodnight, Mr. Murphy, and thank you for an illuminating afternoon."

There was no reason to do it other than his own suspicious nature and his experience with the law, but when he was alone in his hotel room, Murphy slipped the folded paper with Kyoto's thumbprint on it out of his jacket pocket.

He grabbed the paper on the way out when no one was watching.

He dug out a pencil and wrote under the thumbprint, *Ren Norio Kyoto, right print thumb.*

He folded the paper and tucked it into his notebook.

From the satchel Murphy grabbed the bottle of his father's whiskey and poured two ounces into a water glass and then sat on the bed to drink it.

And wondered why he didn't trust Kyoto.

CHAPTER NINE

Boyle needed to stretch his legs and Murphy took the west road out of Dodge City following the railroad tracks.

The job of connecting Dodge with the Santa Fe line had been completed months ago and there were no signs of the once-thriving railroad camp where he first met Sally Orr.

Just flatlands and desert.

He rode Boyle about three miles and dismounted.

There was nothing to see, but he approximated the site where he last marked the railroad camp.

Every fence and post had been removed. Every tent and evidence that hundreds of people lived and worked here for months had vanished.

Murphy dismounted and rubbed Boyle's long, powerful neck.

He dug some sugar cubes out of a pocket

and fed them to Boyle.

"When we get home, whenever that might be, I'll tell Burke this was our last job," he told Boyle as the horse ate from his hand.

"Both of us are getting too damn old to be traveling around the country as errand boys when we have a home and a bed and a woman like Sally waiting for us," Murphy said.

Boyle licked the last granules of sugar off his hand.

"Let's go a few more miles just to stretch our legs," Murphy said and mounted Boyle.

Marshal Adams was sitting in a chair on the porch of the Dodge Hotel when Murphy returned riding Boyle.

Adams had a cup of coffee and a rolled cigarette.

Murphy dismounted and tied Boyle to the hitching post.

"Been waiting for you," Adams said. "Got a package for you from a William Burke in Washington."

Murphy took the stairs to the porch, looked at the box beside Adams, and took the vacant seat next to him.

"Ride anywhere special?" Adams said.

"Three months ago I tracked a serial killer to the railroad camp when they were connecting Dodge to Santa Fe," Murphy said. "I needed to stretch my horse's legs and took a ride out there. It's all gone."

"Been gone for months now," Adams said. "I heard they had a big party in town to celebrate and then moved on."

"I last heard they were expanding the A&P to include Oregon and Washington territory," Murphy said.

"I heard the same. I have to go to Topeka to pick up a prisoner headed for Yuma," Adams said. "Be gone a week. Will you be here when I get back?"

Murphy glanced at the package. "Doubtful."

Adams stood and extended his right hand.

Murphy stood and they shook.

"Good luck," Adams said.

"You, too."

After delivering Boyle to the livery, Murphy took the package to his room. He filled a glass with his father's whiskey, loaded his pipe, and opened the package.

The first thing he saw was the letter from Sally.

A quick rush of excitement ran through him at seeing the sealed envelope with his name written in her handwriting.

He decided to save the letter for later, set

it on the nightstand, and removed the files from the box.

He lifted the file marked, **Forgers and known counter-feiters released from prison the past five years.**

Bruce Logan. Age fifty-nine. Arrested for producing counterfeit money after the war in 1867. Sentenced to fifteen years. Released after ten when he was diagnosed with a form of terminal cancer of the lungs. Still alive. Lives in a hospital for tuberculosis patients in Arizona near Phoenix.

Derek Parker. Age thirty-nine. Sentenced to ten years at Yuma for producing counter-feit money in 1866. Released four years ago. Last known residence Kansas City, Kansas.

Richard Coy. Age fifty-one. Sentenced to fifteen years at Yuma for producing counter-feit money in 1867. Served ten. Last known residence in Lawrence, Texas.

Three convicted counterfeiters died in Leavenworth and two were shot and killed during prison escapes.

Burke's notes: Seven counterfeiters still incarcerated in various prisons not due for release, earliest 1883.

Known counterfeiters still at large.

Little Johnny Boston. Age sixty-three.

Whereabouts unknown. Last seen in Nevada in 1877. Believed to have died.

Willie Robbie. Age forty-seven. Whereabouts unknown. Last seen in Utah by a US Marshal.

Murphy closed the file and picked up the next one.

Ink suppliers for US currency.

Saint Louis Ink Supply Company. Supplies ink to US Govt. for printing currency. Formula is kept secret and not made for anyone. Supplies ink to forty-one newspapers in west, midwest, and west coast.

Philadelphia Ink. Supplies ink to US Govt. for printing currency east coast and forty-three newspapers on east coast as far west as Chicago. Formula for ink kept secret.

San Francisco Wholesale Ink Supply Co. Supplies ink to US mint located in San Francisco. Supplies ink to fifty-seven newspapers as far west as Kansas.

Murphy closed the file and opened the final folder.

Retired from government service as engravers.

Eleven men retired in the past five years.

Nine on east coast. Checked out by Secret Service. Two on west coast unaccounted for as yet.

Harvey Lutz. Age sixty-three. San Francisco.

Paul Lee. Age fifty-seven. Portland, Or.

Murphy closed the file and picked up the report written in Burke's handwriting.

Tools made for US Government for engravers to use are made by several government contracted tool & dye companies. Tools are made to specific standards and not duplicated for private use. Engravers do not own the tools they use and must account for them at the end of their work day. Tools that are worn are destroyed. New tools are made only by request by Sect. of Treasury Office.

Sheets for imprinting currency are made at the mint using heavy metal presses and metal alloy of secret formula. Amount of pressure is kept secret and known only to press operators.

Murphy set the note aside and sipped some of his father's whiskey. He dumped the spent tobacco from his pipe into the tin ashtray on the nightstand, refilled the bowl, lit it, and sipped more whiskey.

He tore open the envelope and removed Sally's letter.

Dearest Murphy,

I didn't believe it possible I could ever miss someone as much as I am missing you now. I have kept busy making lists and packing and Mr. Burke has been most helpful making arrangements with a shipping company to transport to Tennessee the things I believe you wish to take. Also, he has helped with the dogs I wish to adopt, a pair of male Danes about ten weeks old. I will bring them home in two weeks. Before I left Saint Louis I liquidated everything I have and converted it to cash and it is in a bank in Washington waiting to be drawn upon. A little more than eighteen-thousand dollars for us to use if the need ever arises. I didn't mention this before because you have a slight stubborn streak in you when it comes to paying the bills. I confided this to Mr. Burke and he joked that it would snow in hell before you ever allowed a woman to pay the bills. And speaking of Mr. Burke, he asked if he may keep a bottle of your father's whiskey and I gave him one. He claimed it was for medicinal purposes. I don't believe him on that one. I have to end this now as he is waiting to take a package to the railroad with this letter included. You have my love, thoughts, and prayers. Sally.

Murphy read the letter a second time and then tucked it away in his satchel.

His stomach moaned and he realized he hadn't had a bite to eat since an early breakfast. He was about to stand and leave the room when there was a knock on the door.

"Mr. Murphy?" a male voice said from the hallway.

Silently, Murphy stood and eased the Peacemaker from its holster, slowly cocking it so it didn't make a sound.

"Who is it?" he said.

"My name is Rogers, sir. I am Miss Ritchie's cook. She's asked me to invite you to dinner at her home tonight, along with Mr. Kyoto."

"What time?"

"Six-thirty for drinks, seven for dinner."

"I'll be there."

"A carriage will pick you up at . . ."

"I'll walk," Murphy said.

"Sir?"

"I'll walk. Thank you."

Murphy waited until he heard the man's footsteps fade away and then de-cocked the Peacemaker and returned it to the holster.

He opened the satchel and removed the suit rolled into a tube and held in place by a belt, removed the belt, and tossed the suit onto the bed.

He looked in the mirror over the dresser.

He gathered up the suit and left the room. In the lobby, he stopped at the front desk to speak to the clerk.

"I'd like a hot bath and a brushing of this suit," Murphy told the desk clerk.

"Three dollars for both," the clerk said.

"Call me in my room when the bath is ready," Murphy said as he removed three one-dollar coins from a pocket.

CHAPTER TEN

"Mr. Kyoto is leaving us on Monday of next week," Mary Kate said as she sipped champagne.

"I'm glad I brought him a gift then," Murphy said.

They were in the parlor room adjacent to the dining room.

Kyoto looked at Murphy.

"A gift?" he said.

As he entered the room a few minutes earlier, Murphy had set a tall sack on the bar table. He picked it up and gave it to Kyoto.

"My father and his father before him are makers of fine bourbon whiskey," Murphy said. "I always travel with at least two bottles."

Kyoto removed the quart bottle from the sack and held it up and the amber liquid glowed in the light of the oil lanterns.

"Bourbon whiskey?" Kyoto said.

"Made from corn and aged in charred oak barrels," Murphy said.

Kyoto bowed slightly.

"I am humbled by your thoughtfulness," Kyoto said.

"It's sipping whiskey, Mr. Kyoto," Murphy said. "Meant to be savored on the tongue one small sip at a time."

"I shall do so," Kyoto said.

Rogers entered the parlor.

"Dinner is ready, Miss Ritchie," he said.

Mary Kate set her champagne glass on a table and took Murphy's right arm in hers and Kyoto's left arm and said, "Shall we?"

"Mr. Kyoto is off to Nebraska to study the feed and grain business," Mary Kate said.

"Yes, I am most anxious to learn American ways of feeding cattle," Kyoto said. "Especially how this is performed during the winter months."

"Nebraska would be the place to learn about corn," Murphy said.

"Your father's whiskey you said is made from corn," Kyoto said.

"Corn for human consumption," Murphy said. "A different type is grown for cattle and livestock."

"I see that I have much to learn," Kyoto said.

"What about you, Mr. Murphy?" Mary Kate said.

"I'll be moving on probably tomorrow."

"To where?"

"I'm afraid that's classified information."

"Your work as a policeman?" Kyoto said.

"Yes."

"Then let's make the most of this last meal together," Mary Kate said.

Murphy shook hands with Kyoto in the front parlor next to the open door.

"Maybe we shall cross paths again, Mr. Murphy," Kyoto said.

"Maybe," Murphy said.

Holding his bottle of bourbon, Kyoto walked to the door and down the steps where his two bodyguards waited beside the carriage. Kyoto's manservant sat in the driver's seat holding the reins.

Murphy looked at Mary Kate.

"Well, Miss Ritchie, thank you for an elegant dinner," he said.

"You don't have to leave just yet," Mary Kate said. "I would like to show you the second floor."

"What's on the second floor?" Murphy said.

"My bedroom."

"I'm afraid I have to leave very early in

the morning," Murphy said.

"Mr. Murphy, what you said the other day about why I'm unmarried, I'm afraid that it's true," Mary Kate. "However, that doesn't mean that sometimes I don't get . . . lonely."

"I understand," Murphy said. "But it took me a very long time to find the right woman and I don't want to do anything she wouldn't approve of."

"Lucky woman," Mary Kate said.

"It's more like the other way around," Murphy said.

CHAPTER ELEVEN

Murphy decided to take the railroad east to Wichita and then north to Topeka and finally northeast to Kansas City, hopefully to talk with Derek Parker. With a bit of luck Parker was still in the area and wouldn't be too difficult to find.

The train arrived fifty minutes later than its scheduled time of ten in the morning. It would have to make up some time to arrive in Wichita at the scheduled time of four in the afternoon.

Finally able to board Boyle in the last car, Murphy entered the riding car, stored his satchel under the seat, and sat down with his notes.

According to reports written by the arresting US Marshals, Derek Parker was a nonviolent man who made a living engraving fine silver and pewter before the war in South Carolina. He fought against the North and when wounded in sixty-four, returned home to nothing. No house, wife, business, not even his dog. He decided to keep fighting the Yankees by producing counterfeit Yankee dollars and notes and spreading them around the west and north.

Murphy could have wired the sheriff in Kansas City, but he didn't want to risk alerting Parker, giving the man cause to flee.

Murphy closed his notebook and tucked it away in his satchel.

There was nothing to do except look out the window and wait for the dining car to open for business.

After lunch in the crowded dining car, Murphy returned to his seat and took a short nap. He awoke around two and went to visit Boyle in the last car. As always, Boyle was happy to see him and he rewarded him with some sugar cubes from the dining car.

"I might as well stay here with you," Murphy said and removed a brush from the saddlebags to brush Boyle's mane.

Sally pulled the plug in the tub and the water drained out through the pipe under the tub to the backyard. The pipe was buried so the water flowed unseen directly into the ground.

She wrapped a towel around her hair and

used a second towel to dry her body. Then she stepped out of the tub and grabbed her robe and slipped it on and tied the belt tightly around her waist.

She decided on a light supper of sandwiches of cold chicken with tea. In the bedroom she put on house slippers and went down to the first floor and froze in place at the sight of Christopher seated in a chair in the kitchen, sipping from a tall glass of whiskey.

From the looks of him it wasn't the first glass.

They made and held eye contact.

"Leave now and I won't tell Murphy about this," Sally said.

Christopher gulped whiskey and grinned. His eyes were bloodshot red.

"Tell him what? That you're a whore?" Christopher said. "I think he already knows that."

Sally glanced at the counter where a block of sharp kitchen knives rested next to the breadbox.

Christopher yanked a .38 revolver from his inside jacket shoulder holster.

"I'd shoot you before you reached it," he said.

Sally removed the towel from her hair and tossed it on the counter. Her blond hair, still wet, fell well past her shoulders.

"What is it you want?" she said.

"What do I want?" Christopher said. He took a sip from his glass. "All those old, shriveled up senators and congressmen I shuffled to your whorehouse last year during that conference in Saint Louis and every time I had to wait in the carriage like a good little boy, never allowed to have a taste of the forbidden fruit. I saw you, though. You didn't see me, but I saw you."

Christopher downed the last of the whiskey and set the glass on the floor.

He stood up and cocked the revolver.

"Now it's my turn to have a taste," he said. "Lose that robe."

Sally didn't move. He was drunk and the .38 was cocked and aimed in her direction.

"I said lose it!" Christopher shouted.

Sally's hands slowly came up to the knot in the belt, untied it, and the robe fell away to the floor.

Christopher stared at her.

His eyes were wide and bloodshot and his intention reflected in them.

Then he staggered slowly forward.

The last thing Sally saw before she closed her eyes was the twisted sneer on his lips.

Murphy walked Boyle off the platform to

the dirt street and paused for a moment to look at Kansas City some three-hundred feet away.

He had been here once before during the war on a scouting party when the population was less than five hundred and the town consisted of five or six streets.

From the train depot the town spread out in all directions and a thousand lights in windows were visible.

The population had grown to around fifteen thousand.

Across the border into Missouri, the town of Independence was less than a day's ride. The Missouri River cut through both states and trade along the river improved commerce before and after the war.

Murphy walked Boyle into town where music from a dozen saloons could be heard even from a distance.

Murphy found the Hotel Kansas City without too much trouble. At four flights, it stood twice as high as most structures in town. They had gotten his wire and held a room for him and a space at their private livery for Boyle.

In his room, Murphy filled a water glass with his father's whiskey, lit his pipe, and opened the third-floor window. The night was hot and the room was stifling. Piano and saloon music filtered in along with the laughter of saloon girls.

Oil lanterns on poles illuminated the wood sidewalks below. A few men staggered in and out of various saloons.

Piano music filled the air.

A typical cowboy town.

He turned away from the window and sat on the bed to finish whiskey and pipe.

He had the urge to write another letter to Sally and he would tomorrow when he was awake and clear-headed. He thought when the job was finished they could get married on the farm. A small wedding with just his parents and a few close friends; she in in a white, wedding dress, he in a fine, black suit.

He thought he'd tell her they both weren't too old yet for a couple of kids, if she was willing.

And now that he put the guilt behind him.

He thought about a proper wedding ring. If he needed to make the trip west to San Francisco, that would be the place to buy one. Known for elegance and its fine stores and shops, he should have little trouble finding a proper ring for Sally.

With that thought in mind, Murphy pulled down the covers of the bed, stripped off his clothes, and fell into a deep, dreamless sleep.

■ ■ ■ ■

Sally opened her eyes to sunlight streaming in through the kitchen window. She was on the floor and cold. He left her naked and unconscious shortly before dawn.

She sat up slowly, feeling dizzy and nauseous.

She held onto a cabinet to pull herself to her feet and then the urge to vomit overcame her and she rushed to the door, opened it, ran down the stairs, and vomited in the backyard grass.

When there was nothing left in her stomach, she returned to the kitchen and ran the pump in the sink and stuck her head under the icy cold water.

The towel was on the counter where she left it and she used it to dry her face and hair. She noticed the rope burns on her wrists where the bastard had tied her hands and she cranked the pump again and washed them with the bar of soap beside the pump.

Then she picked up her robe, slipped it on, and tied the belt.

Tobacco pouch and paper were on the counter and she rolled a cigarette and lit it with a wood match. The smoke was harsh and burned her throat, but calmed her down in the process.

She sat at the table and noticed the dried blood under her fingernails.

When he came at her she had tried to run, but he grabbed her hair and slapped her across the face. Then he forced her down to the floor and . . .

She'd scratched his face with her fingernails.

He didn't seem to notice the blood on his cheeks and he pinned her down with his weight and . . .

When he was finished that's when he tied her hands and ankles.

And fixed a couple of cold chicken sandwiches and sat at the table to eat them and drink more whiskey.

Until he was ready to have a second go-round.

Her ankles?

There were rope burns on them as well.

At least the son of a bitch didn't leave her hog-tied when he was done with her.

When the cigarette burned her fingers, Sally realized that she had been staring into space.

She felt dirty and violated and in need of a bath.

She ran the pump and filled several basins

and made a fire in the stove to boil the water for the tub.

Murphy had breakfast at a restaurant a few blocks from the hotel. After he ate he went looking for the sheriff's office. Kansas City had an elected town sheriff named Bart Goodwin and a county sheriff named Roscoe Woodward.

Goodwin's jurisdiction ended one-hundred yards outside of town. Woodward's began at the town line and encompassed the entire county. Woodward could serve as backup to Goodwin if and when needed.

Woodward was out of town on county business. Across the wide, dirt street, Goodwin was at his desk drinking coffee. Two town deputies were also drinking coffee, but standing.

Goodwin and his deputies froze in place when Murphy opened the door and entered the office.

One of the deputies placed his hand over his gun butt and slid off the lash.

"Don't do that," Murphy said. "It makes me nervous and could make you dead."

Goodwin looked at his deputy. "Drink your coffee," he said.

"Name is Murphy. I wired you from Dodge City," Murphy said.

"I got it," Goodwin said. "Can you prove who you are?"

"If I can reach for my wallet without your deputy drawing down on me," Murphy said.

"Go ahead," Goodwin said.

Murphy dug out his folding wallet and set it on the desk.

Goodwin picked it up, opened it, and then handed it back to Murphy.

"Boys, this is Mr. Murphy," he said. "US Secret Service Agent here on official federal business."

"What business is that?" one of the deputies said.

"Mr. Derek Parker," Murphy said.

"Derek . . . the squirrely guy who runs the printing press at the newspaper?" the deputy asked.

"Is there another Derek Parker in town?" Murphy said.

"No."

"Sheriff, I'd appreciate it if you accompanied me to talk to him," Murphy said.

"If I know why," Goodwin said.

"How long has Parker lived in town?" Murphy said.

"Two years, maybe a bit more," Goodwin said. "Has a young wife and a baby boy."

"Did you know he spent ten years in federal prison for producing counterfeit money?" Murphy asked.

"I knew he was in prison and I know he paid his debt, but I didn't know it was for counterfeiting money," Goodwin said. "Do you think he's doing it again? Is that why you're here?"

"Thousands of dollars in counterfeit bills have turned up in stores and banks," Murphy said. "I'm just following leads. Care to accompany me?"

"I will," Goodwin said. He looked at his deputies. "Go on patrol."

After a long hot bath, Sally stood before Murphy's dressing mirror and inspected her face and body.

Her left eye was severely blackened. Both lips were swollen and bruised. Choke marks encircled her neck. Rope burns were on ankles and wrists.

She wouldn't be presentable in public for weeks.

Murphy told her to take the rifle with her everywhere that she went, but to the bathtub?

Sally stared at her reflection in the mirror.

Then sank to her knees and buried her face in her hands and cried.

Murphy and Goodwin entered the office of

the *Kansas City Gazette* and a little bell rang when the door opened and closed.

The editor of the paper, a small man named Banks, looked up from his desk at Goodwin.

"Sheriff," he said. "What can I do for you?"

"Derek Parker around?" Goodwin said.

"Pressroom. Why?"

"Just some questions is all," Goodwin said.

And a door slamming shut from the pressroom alerted Murphy and Goodwin.

Murphy and Goodwin walked to the pressroom door and Murphy grabbed the knob and yanked the door open.

Beyond the printing press was an open back door.

Murphy and Goodwin rushed to the door and stepped outside to the edge of town where Derek Parker was running toward nothing but wide open spaces.

"Where does he think he's going on foot?" Murphy said.

"Feel like chasing him?" Goodwin asked.

"No."

Parker had run about a hundred feet and didn't appear to want to slow down.

Murphy pulled his Peacemaker and fired three shots into the dirt directly behind Parker.

"That's enough of this running crap, Parker," Murphy shouted.

Parker came to a stop, put his hands on his head, turned around, and shrugged his shoulders at Murphy.

Murphy holstered the Peacemaker.

Derek Parker sipped coffee and looked at the counterfeit bills Murphy set before him on the table.

After leaving the newspaper, Murphy took Parker and Goodwin to the dining room at his hotel and ordered coffee for all three.

Parker inspected a twenty-dollar note. He held it to the light, then sideways, and rubbed the paper between thumb and forefinger.

"Damn fine work," he said.

"First rate," Murphy said.

"Not even a hit of the devil's cut," Parker said.

"The what?" Goodwin said.

"Devil's cut," Parker said.

"My father has made whiskey for forty years," Murphy said. "It ages in oak barrels for years before it mellows enough to drink. Some evaporates over time through the wood. They call that the devil's cut."

"When a skilled counterfeiter cuts the bills with a paper cutter he sometimes doesn't line the paper up with the guide evenly," Parker said. "The edges turn out slightly uneven. The edge that's smaller than the other we call the devil's cut. This bill is as close to perfect as possible for counterfeit."

Goodwin picked up a bill. "Can you make this?" he said to Parker.

"Not anymore," Parker said. "A decade of hard labor has ruined my hands. My knuckles are swollen and I have arthritis in six of ten fingers."

Parker held up his hands to show the swollen, slightly gnarled fingers.

"You need the skill of a surgeon and the fingers of a pianist to carve the intricate details on a tin sheet to prepare a proper plate," Parker said. "And all the skill in the world doesn't matter if your hands are ruined."

"What about the press at the paper?" Goodwin asked.

"Too small, not enough pressure," Parker said. He looked at Murphy. "Right, Mr. Murphy?"

Murphy nodded as he sipped some coffee.

Goodwin turned to Murphy.

"You figured all along Parker here was innocent of this?" he said.

"More or less," Murphy said.

"Well for Christ sake, Parker, why did you run like that?" Goodwin said.

Parker sipped coffee before answering. "I took one look at Mr. Murphy through the glass window between the shop and office and I knew what he was here for," he said. "I spent ten years at Yuma busting rocks and I don't fancy anymore. I got a new wife, a baby son, and a job that pays fifteen a week and a penny bonus on every handbill I print for every business in town and county. Some months I make an extra ten or twelve dollars in bonus money. I have a good twenty years left in me that I don't want to spend busting rocks. I panicked. That's why I ran."

"Understandable," Murphy said. "One final question. Do you know anybody capable of doing such fine detail as this note?"

Parker sighed and picked up the twenty-dollar note again. He dug out the printer's magnifying glass he always kept in his shirt pocket and inspected the note carefully.

"Best work I've ever seen," he said, setting the note down. "Better than I could ever do. I met a man, Richard Coy, in Yuma. He was a counterfeiter like me only better. He carved an exact picture of the prison interior on a flat rock he found in the yard using a pick he stole from the prison dentist. He

121

might be capable of work as good as this before they sent him up, but I don't know about now."

"Thanks for your time," Murphy said.

Parker nodded and stood up from the table.

"Hey, what would you have done if I didn't stop?" he asked.

"I would have shot you right in the ass," Murphy said.

"How many banks you have in town?" Murphy said as he and Goodwin walked back to Goodwin's office.

"Two. One belongs to the Cattlemen's Association."

"Walk over with me," Murphy said. "I need to tell them to do a full audit of all cash on hand."

"They won't like that," Goodwin said.

Murphy grinned. "They never do."

CHAPTER TWELVE

Burke ordered a carriage to take him to Congress and requested Christopher as the driver. He was disappointed when it wasn't Christopher handling the reins. Christopher was to be appointed one of three drivers for the president and Burke wanted to tell him of this honor himself.

"Where is Mr. Christopher?" Burke asked as he boarded the carriage.

"Out sick today, Mr. Burke," the driver said. "I'm afraid he had a bit too much to drink last night at some downtown pub and got into a bit of a scrape."

"Is he all right?"

"He said he just needed to sleep it off."

Burke nodded. "Take me to Congress."

Sally soaked in a hot tub full of salts and perfumes to try to wash away some of the soreness. Two days after being roughed up by that pig and her body still felt like she'd

123

gone twenty rounds with John L. Sullivan.

In another day or so, the soreness, aches, and pains would be gone, but the question on her mind was what to do about it?

Could she keep it to herself and never tell Murphy?

Never tell anybody?

Put it behind her as if it never happened and continue on with the plans she and Murphy made to move to Tennessee?

What would Murphy do if she told him?

He would kill him.

No questions asked.

That's what Murphy would do.

They found not a single counterfeit bill in either bank. It was a pretty sure bet the stores and shopkeepers hadn't taken in a false bill or note or they would be at the banks by now.

It was time to move on.

Over breakfast at the hotel dining room, Murphy studied his notes, maps, and train schedules.

He decided to go south to Lawrence, Texas, to check out Richard Coy before going west to Arizona.

After breakfast, Murphy returned to his room, packed his satchel and small suitcase, and returned to the lobby to check out.

As he descended the stairs and entered the lobby, Murphy was surprised to see Kyoto's manservant at the desk.

Murphy waited for the little man to finish his business and turn around before Murphy made eye contact and said, "Mr. Kyoto's manservant, aren't you?"

The manservant bowed.

"What are you doing here?" Murphy said.

"Mr. Kyoto will arrive later tonight by train on the way to Omaha," he said softly and in near perfect English. "He sent me ahead to book rooms and make arrangements."

Murphy nodded. "What is your name?"

"Ito."

"Well, Mr. Ito, give Mr. Kyoto my best."

Ito nodded and politely turned away and left the lobby.

After checking out and retrieving Boyle, Murphy stopped by Goodwin's office.

"Leaving us?" Goodwin said.

"Following the leads," Murphy said. "Tonight, a Mr. Kyoto will arrive by train. He's a Japanese diplomat studying the cattle business in America. He's on the up-and-up as far as I can tell, but you might want to greet him personally at the railroad just to keep him out of trouble. Most people in these parts have never seen a Japanese man and his crew before. He travels with two bodyguards and a servant. The servant is over at the hotel booking rooms."

"Thanks for the tip," Goodwin said. "Maybe I'll see you again."

The closest the railroad could take Murphy to Lawrence, Texas, was Dallas. Boyle needed a good stretch of the legs after spending so much time enclosed in a boxcar, so he would ride the two-day trip to Lawrence.

The ride to Dallas was scheduled at thirty-six hours, so Murphy booked a sleeping car rather than try to sleep sitting up in a hard chair in a commuter car.

Around noon, Murphy went for lunch in the dining car and read a copy of the *Kansas City Star* while he ate a steak.

After lunch he retired to his sleeper car, filled his pipe and a glass with his father's whiskey, and broke out pencil and paper to compose a letter to Sally.

Burke sat at the desk in his private office in the White House and stewed over the Christopher incident.

A man appointed driver to the president needed to show more decorum than drunken bar fights and missed days at work

126

because of hangovers.

He dug out the notebook where he kept addresses of all employees and checked Christopher's. He lived about a mile and a half from the White House.

Burke checked with the president's secretary to see if he was needed and then left the White House and grabbed a vacant carriage. He drove himself to the address listed as Christopher's residence.

Christopher lived on a busy street in a less than well-to-do neighborhood. It was always amazing to Burke how just such a short distance from the inner circle of the White House, the money seemed to dwindle with each passing block.

Christopher's flat was on the third floor of a wood-slat apartment building four-flights high.

Burke parked the carriage and entered the building through a lobby that smelled of stale urine and vomit and climbed the three flights to Christopher's apartment door. There were three apartments to a floor and his was listed as 3B.

Burke knocked loudly. Behind the door, Burke heard a noise and then Christopher said, "Yeah, who is it?"

"William Burke."

And the door opened.

Christopher wore a ratty robe and slippers. He was a mess. His hair was unkempt and long scratch marks covered both sides of his face.

"My God, what happened to you?" Burke asked, slightly taken aback by his appearance.

"Come in," Christopher said.

Burke entered and Christopher closed the door.

"Had a few too many pints at a pub last night and the rest is a blur," Christopher said.

"Your face," Christopher said.

"I know."

"Somebody scratched you."

"Like I said, I don't remember," Christopher said. "I don't even remember how I got home. I was celebrating a friend's birthday and well . . ."

"Besides the scratches, are you hurt?"

"Not really," Christopher said. "A few bumps and bruises, but nothing that will keep me away from work after today."

"That's good, because I have some rather good news," Burke said.

Murphy sealed the five-page letter to Sally and tucked it into his jacket pocket so he wouldn't forget to post it in Dallas.

He took his notebook and left the room for the dining car. Too early for dinner, he ordered a pot of coffee and flipped pages and read his notes on Richard Coy. Parker said he was the best he'd ever seen and engraved an image of the Yuma Prison on a rock using a dentist pick.

The skill level to do such high-quality work as the counterfeit bills displayed was still there in Coy's fingers.

But, was the desire?

Murphy flipped through his notes.

Two counterfeiters were still at large. Little Johnny Boston and Willie Robbie.

Two retired engravers, one in San Francisco, one in Portland, Oregon.

He could be gone from home another month or even longer and if that was the case, he would make arrangements to spend some time with Sally in Tennessee, possibly before heading to San Francisco.

They could settle into his old house and make it theirs before he headed west again. Maybe they could even squeeze a trip over to see his father? He hadn't seen the old man for a while and he wouldn't live forever.

He would write another letter to Burke asking him to ride to Tennessee with Sally when she was ready to make the trip.

Murphy left the dining car and went to

visit Boyle, to give him some sugar cubes and a much-needed brushing.

"I was thinking," Murphy said as he fed cubes to Boyle, "how good the front porch of our Tennessee home looks this time of year."

Boyle snorted and licked the last bit of sugar off Murphy's hand.

"And your biggest problem will be which filly to cozy up to," Murphy said.

He took a brush off the shelf in the boxcar and started brushing Boyle's thick mane and shoulders.

"We'll do some riding when we get to Dallas," Murphy said. "We have to keep you fit and trim for the ladies."

Boyle snorted.

"And I'll tell you something else," Murphy said. "I miss my lady."

Boyle turned his head and snorted again.

"Exactly right," Murphy said.

CHAPTER THIRTEEN

Burke set out for Murphy's house driving the carriage himself. He wanted to check on Sally's progress with the planned move before he reserved a freight company that specialized in relocating families.

The Great Danes would be ready to adopt soon and there was that consideration to take into account.

Burke arrived at Murphy's farmhouse and parked the carriage by the porch. He climbed the steps to the porch and knocked on the door.

"Sally, it's William Burke," he said.

After a few seconds of silence, he knocked again, louder.

"Sally, it's William Burke," he said louder. "Are you in there, Sally?"

He heard her footsteps and then the door opened.

Sally was wrapped in a robe with the collar turned up. Her hair was down and her

131

face was pale as if she was ill.

"Sally, what is the . . . ?" Burke said.

And Sally fell into his arms and burst into tears.

Dallas, Texas, was a sprawling town of about ten-thousand residents. Founded along the Trinity River, the area the town was built upon was flat and bland in appearance.

While neighboring Fort Worth was quickly becoming a hub for stockyards and the beef industry, Dallas was more prone to the farming community. Cotton gin mill machinery and other such modern industrial machinery were produced on a large scale, as well as cotton itself.

That's how Murphy saw it as he walked Boyle from the railroad station to the hotel in the center of town on Main Street. The streets were busy with pedestrians, wagons, and cowboys on horseback. Stores and shops seemed to be everywhere and everybody seemed to be in one big hurry. It reminded him of Washington.

After checking into the hotel, Murphy asked where the sheriff's office was located. He walked Boyle to the livery and then traveled ten blocks along wood-plank sidewalks to the sheriff's office.

The hard-looking man behind the desk

looked at Murphy when, holding his Winchester rifle in his left hand, he opened the door and walked into the sheriff's office.

"Are you the sheriff?" Murphy said.

"Tom Downs, who are you?"

"Name is Murphy."

Murphy dug out his wallet, opened it, and handed it across the desk to Downs.

"Secret Service?" Downs said.

"I just got off the train," Murphy said. "I'd like some coffee. Want to get a cup of coffee with me?"

"For God's sake, Sally, tell me who did this to you?" Burke asked.

They were drinking tea in the kitchen.

"Does it matter?" Sally said. "It's over and done with. Why talk about it?"

"There are laws against . . ."

"Against what?" Sally said. "Have him arrested and take the stand in court. Tell the whole world that the woman Murphy wants to marry is nothing but a common madam of a whorehouse. A jury will look at the respectable man on trial and his whore accuser and reach what conclusion? And when the respectable man goes free what do you think Murphy will do then?"

Burke stared at her.

Sally patted his hand.

"I lost control earlier, but I'm all right now," she said. "And this must be kept just between us. Promise me that, Mr. Burke."

Burke stared at Sally.

"Promise," she said.

"Yes, all right, I promise."

Sally nodded. "More tea?"

"Please."

Sally lifted the teapot and filled Burke's cup.

That's when Burke noticed how chipped and jagged her fingernails were compared to their usual polished, smooth appearance.

"Sally, I almost forgot the reason for my visit," Burke said. "The Danes."

"Yeah, I know Richard Coy," Downs said. "Everybody around here does. Has a small place west of town in the foothills of Lawrence. In my opinion the man is crazy."

"How so?" Murphy said.

They were in a small café a few storefronts down from Downs's office. Each had a ceramic mug of coffee.

"He showed up here early in seventy-eight with five-hundred dollars in his pocket and the first thing he does is buy the old Potter shack west of town and two mules," Downs said.

"Mules? What for?"

"Crude oil," Downs said. "He's convinced Texas is full of crude oil and he's determined to find it."

Murphy sipped some coffee and said, "Is it?"

"Full of crude oil, how would I know?" Downs said. "And even if it were, what good is the filthy stuff anyway?"

"How far out of town is he?" Murphy said.

"Six or seven miles west toward Lawrence."

Murphy pulled out his pocket watch. It was just after ten o'clock.

"Care to ride with me out to Coy's place?" he said.

"Was Coy pardoned or paroled?" Downs said.

"Presidential pardon," Murphy said. "By that idiot Hayes."

"I take it you don't approve of pardons."

"A parole is one thing, but a pardon is like the crime never happened."

They were a mile or so from Coy's cabin on the foothills.

"If he was such a threat to the government, why did Hayes pardon him?" Downs said.

"You'd have to take that up with Hayes," Murphy said. "Personally, the only one I

135

had any use for was Grant."

"I hear he's on some kind of speaking tour around the country."

"And Europe."

A loud explosion in the distance caused Murphy and Downs to stop their horses.

"What the hell was that?" Murphy asked.

"That would be Richard Coy."

"That came from the northwest."

"Then that's where he probably is," Downs said.

Burke found Christopher having a pint in a seedy pub a few blocks from his apartment building.

Christopher was alone with his pint and smoking a rolled cigarette when Burke sat down uninvited.

"Mr. Burke," Christopher said. "Two visits in one day."

"Please tell me that you aren't stupid enough to molest Murphy's woman," Burke said.

Christopher stared at Burke.

"I've seen the bruises on her and I've seen her fingernails," Burke said. "She scratched your face with those nails when you . . . accosted her."

"She's nothing but a common whore," Christopher said. "No different than the whores I shuffle the fat cats to here in Washington. I saw her once in Saint Louis. Same deal, sit in the carriage like a good little boy and wait while those congressmen had their fun. Well, no more. Besides, what can she do, claim innocence?"

"She can tell Murphy, that's what she can do," Burke said.

"Relax. Have a drink," Christopher said. "How bad would it make the president seem in the eyes of the press and Congress if a member of his staff, and I give you the fact that I'm just a driver but a member of his staff nonetheless, but how bad a reflection on the president would it be if I were accused of what you're accusing me of? Besides, what's worse in the eyes of the law, roughing up a common whore or murdering the president's personal driver?"

Burke waved a girl over and asked her for a shot of whiskey. She set a shot glass on the table, filled it, and walked away.

Burke lifted the glass and tossed back the shot. It was harsh, rough whiskey.

"Let me tell you something about Murphy," Burke said. "He is the best regulator in the business and he answers to only one law. His own. And that's what you should be concerned about, and only that."

Murphy and Downs turned northwest at Coy's cabin and rode several miles, stopping when they not only heard but saw another explosion several hundred yards in front of them.

"Damn fool," Downs said as he tried to calm his horse.

Boyle, used to gunfire and loud explosions, took it in stride as Murphy dismounted.

"Coy? Richard Coy?" Murphy shouted.

Downs dismounted and held the reins tightly.

"Richard Coy?" Murphy shouted.

Several rifle shots sounded and the bullets hit the ground in front of Murphy. Downs threw himself on the ground as his horse ran a hundred feet or more away. Murphy and Boyle stood motionless.

"Don't make me come get you," Murphy said. "And quit wasting your bullets. We both know you're not going to shoot me."

Downs looked up at Murphy.

" 'Quit wasting bullets,' is that what you said?" Downs asked.

Richard Coy stepped out from behind a large rock a hundred feet from Murphy. He had long hair past his shoulders and a thick, bushy beard speckled with gray. He held a Henry rifle in his right hand.

"You ain't after my crude, are you?" Coy asked.

"No," Murphy said.

Coy looked at Downs.

"What are you doing on the ground?" Coy said.

"Richard Coy, we need to have a talk," Murphy said.

"About lunchtime anyway," Coy said. "Got a rabbit stew on the pot back at the cabin. Got plenty. You're welcome to join me."

Murphy ran a piece of hard, crusty bread into the metal tin plate to sop up the last bit of gravy and then bit into it. "Best rabbit stew I've had in years," he said.

"I'd have to agree," Downs said.

"I was a cook in Yuma the last four years," Coy said. "You pick things up as you go along. Coffee?"

"Sure," Murphy said.

Coy went to the stone fireplace where the coffee pot hung suspended over a fire and brought it to the table. He filled three tin mugs and sat.

"Now what's all this bull crap about

counterfeit money?" Coy added sugar from a bowl to his cup.

Murphy dug out several counterfeit bills and set them on the table.

Coy picked up the twenty-dollar note.

He inspected it carefully and then looked at Murphy.

"Best damn work I've seen in twenty years," he said.

"Can you do this kind of work?" Murphy said.

"If I had the right tools, the plates, a model to work from, paper, ink and a press, and a year to do nothing else, yes," Coy said.

"Let me see that," Downs said.

Coy passed him the bill.

"The paper is no good and that ink will never quite dry properly, especially in a wet climate or excessive heat, but it would fool just about anybody who doesn't know better," Coy said. "Bankers, too, I expect."

"It did," Murphy said.

"And you come all this way to see if I was printing money out here in my shack," Coy said with amusement.

"No, not really," Murphy said.

"Then what?"

"I go where the leads take me," Murphy said. "And while I was here I thought I'd ask you if you knew anybody capable of such work."

"Besides me you mean."

"Besides you," Murphy said.

"Met a fellow in Yuma, but his hands went bad from busting rocks," Coy said. "Thing is, in order to make such a bill as this one you need to have a grubstake and a pretty damn good one at that. And resources. Lots of resources."

"Grubstake?" Downs said as he set the bill on the table.

"For the right tools, metal plates or sheets, rolls of paper, ink, and a damn good press," Coy said. "It will set you back a tidy sum all right before the first bill is even printed."

"So you'd need a fair amount of resources to do this?" Downs said.

"I'd say a cost of thirty cents on the dollar," Coy said. "And if sold to the right people for fifty cents on the dollar leaves a profit of twenty cents."

"Twenty cents don't seem worth the trouble," Downs said.

"I agree if you only make one bill," Coy said. "But what if you made a million, five million, or even ten? What's it worth then?"

Downs looked at Murphy.

"Got any more coffee?" Murphy said.

Murphy, Coy, and Downs stood at the edge

141

of a deep pool of black crude oil.

"You blasted this hole?" Downs asked.

Coy nodded. "It's a might tricky," he said. "You want to open the hole up to let the crude seep out and even a slight miscalculation can do the opposite and shut her down."

"Where did you learn to do this?" Murphy said.

"Last six years in Yuma my cellmate was a geologist," Coy said. "We had plenty of time to exchange trade secrets."

"So what good is this foul-smelling stuff?" Downs asked.

"For one thing, making kerosene and lantern oil," Coy said. "And lubricant for machine parts. The more of this stuff you find the less need for killing whales for oil. Some people say this crude will one day power machines to do more work in one hour than a horse could do in a week."

"This stuff?" Downs said.

Murphy knelt down and picked up a twig off the ground. He dipped the twig into the oil and then sniffed it and stood up. He pulled out his matches, struck one, and touched the flame to the twig. It immediately burst into flames.

"Very much like earthquake oil," Murphy said and dropped the twig and extinguished it under his boot.

"Except I made the earthquake myself," Coy said.

"How much of this is under there?" Downs said.

Coy grinned. "An ocean."

Murphy and Downs arrived back in Dallas shortly before sundown.

"Buy you a steak?" Murphy asked as they dismounted in front of Downs's office.

"Why not," Downs said.

"You pick the place," Murphy said.

Burke sat in his office until well after his staff left for the day. He had a bottle of Murphy's father's whiskey in a bottom desk drawer and he took it out and poured a few ounces into a water glass.

He took a sip and lit a long cigar.

The stupid son of a bitch really put him in a tough spot. Sally probably wouldn't tell Murphy what happened for fear of what Murphy would do.

Namely put a bullet in Christopher's stupid head.

If Sally could keep it a secret, so could Burke.

Except that if the story ever broke that the president's personal carriage driver was a rapist there would be hell to pay in the media.

Women were stronger than men when it came to hiding their emotions and dealing with hardship. Burke believed that. Mostly because women had to take so much shit from men during their lifetime.

So Burke was convinced Sally could live forty more years and never say one word to Murphy about Christopher.

But was that the right thing to do?

Exposing the president to potential political disaster and possibly criminal charges loomed heavily on Burke's mind.

And allow a man who should be whipped and jailed to walk free and possibly beat and rape another woman he deemed unfit.

He sipped whiskey, smoked his cigar, and waited for his conscience to guide him to do the right thing.

His conscience and another glass of Murphy's father's whiskey.

"How many banks in town?" Murphy asked as he cut into his steak.

"Let's see," Downs said. "There's the First Bank of Dallas. The Grange Savings and Loan. The Cattlemen's Bank, and the Chicago Trust for industrial loans."

They were having dinner at the restaurant

in Murphy's hotel.

"That's more time than I'd like to spend here, but I'll need the banks to audit their cash in the morning," Murphy said.

"For counterfeit money?" Downs said.

Murphy nodded as he sliced off another piece of steak.

"They won't like that," Downs said. "Having to do all that extra work."

"I haven't met one yet that did," Murphy said.

CHAPTER FOURTEEN

Murphy walked Boyle to the railroad station where he would board the noon train to Phoenix, Arizona.

Downs walked beside Murphy and smoked a rolled cigarette.

"How do you figure almost a thousand dollars in fake money slipped into the banks?" Downs asked. "Right under their noses."

"Money flows into and out of towns, banks, and stores like water," Murphy said. "Most are trained to count it, change it, and store it, but very few are trained to spot the counterfeit from the real."

"I'll send it along to Washington to that address you gave me," Downs said.

"I almost forgot," Murphy said. He dug the letter to Sally out of his jacket pocket and gave it to Downs. "Could you post this for me?"

"Sure."

At the depot, they shook hands.

"Hope to see you again," Downs said.

"One never knows," Murphy said.

Sally read Murphy's latest letter three times from a chair on the porch facing the sun. It was hot and she drank a glass of cool lemonade as she read.

By now Murphy would be in Phoenix, Arizona, or thereabouts.

He said he would take a break in a few weeks and meet her in Tennessee for a week or so of relaxation.

Well, she had much to do to get things packed and shipped to Murphy's Tennessee home.

And the dogs.

She needed to pick up the Danes and get them acclimated to having a home and owner before she went south.

Sally folded the letter and stood up and immediately felt slightly dizzy. She held onto the porch railing to steady her legs until the dizzy spell passed.

Too much sitting in the hot sun, she reasoned, and when she felt better, Sally went inside to finish preparing her very long list of things to do.

Murphy ate breakfast in the dining room of

the Phoenix Hotel and read a copy of the local newspaper, *The Gazette.*

From what Murphy saw of Arizona Territory on the train ride most of the area around the town was nothing but arid desert lands, so what was there to write about in a newspaper?

And statehood, that was decades away from what Murphy understood.

Murphy finished breakfast, paid the bill, left the newspaper, and stepped outside and into the unbearable, bone-dry heat.

He walked a few storefronts down Main Street and entered a general store.

A bald man in a white apron looked at Murphy from behind a counter.

"I need a large canteen," Murphy said. "A gallon if you have one."

"Don't blame you," the man said. "It's a hundred degrees already."

"I thought New Mexico was bad," Murphy said.

"Where you headed?" the man said.

"The hospital north of here to visit a friend."

"Eight miles each way in this heat."

"I know it."

"That sun will blind you," the man said. "Best get a pair of these dark glasses to protect your eyes. Only six bits a pair."

■ ■ ■ ■

Wearing round, rimless dark glasses and carrying a new gallon capacity canteen, Murphy walked to the livery stable at the edge of town where Boyle had spent the night.

The livery manager was on duty.

"Have you a horse used to this sun and heat I could rent for the day?" Murphy asked. "I'd rather not wear mine out. He's not acclimated to this climate."

"Where you riding to?" the manager asked.

"The hospital north of here and back."

"I can let you have Bo for ten dollars, but if something happens to him I have to charge you thirty for the loss and extra for damages to the saddle."

"Can you have him ready in thirty minutes?"

Murphy made the eight-mile trip to the hospital in just under two hours. To say that Bo knew how to ride and protect his hide in one-hundred-degree heat and a blistering sun was an understatement.

The hospital was set back on a hill that overlooked a tributary of the Salt River.

As Murphy dismounted Bo and tied him to a post outside the hospital, he noted the lush gardens and green grass surrounding the large hospital. Either they found a way to pump large amounts of water from the river to the hospital grounds, or somebody spent a great deal of time with a bucket.

The hospital was for people suffering from tuberculosis, asthma, and other serious upper-respiratory illnesses where a dry climate was needed for their survival, and a climate didn't get any drier than Arizona.

Murphy knew that the chances of ever checking out of such a hospital were about the same as beating the house on a roulette wheel. Slim to none.

He entered the hospital lobby. It was decked out with fine furniture, rugs, and desert plants in red clay pots.

A nurse in a crisp white uniform, including hat, greeted Murphy.

"I'm here to see Bruce Logan," Murphy said.

"Are you a family member or friend?" she asked.

"Neither," Murphy said and showed her his identification.

"Mr. Logan is a very sick man," a smug doctor told Murphy. "If I were to guess, I would estimate his life span at a few more months. Please try not to upset him."

"What difference would it make if I do?" Murphy asked.

The doctor resisted the temptation to scold Murphy and escorted him to the fourth-floor ward for tuberculosis patients. There were forty beds separated by forty curtains with five nurses assigned to the ward.

Bruce Logan was in bed number seventeen.

The doctor parted the curtains and allowed Murphy to enter.

"How are you feeling today, Mr. Logan?" the doctor asked.

At least six feet tall, Logan's weight was down to around one hundred and thirty pounds. His flesh was loose and hung off him like deflated sacks. His skin was ashen in color.

Logan looked at the doctor and nodded.

Murphy could hear the hard labor in Logan's breathing.

"This is Mr. Murphy," the doctor said. "He is with the Secret Service and he would like to ask you a few questions. Okay?"

"Why is it if I were a sick, old dog you would put me out of my misery with a bullet to the brain because it's the humane thing to do, but because I'm a man I must suffer this intolerable pain until I die a horrible wretched death?" Logan said, rasping nearly every word.

"Life is a precious gift, Mr. Logan," the doctor said.

"That depends on which side of this bed you're on," Logan said.

The doctor sighed. "I'll check on you later," he said and went outside the curtain.

"And you want?" Logan asked Murphy.

"I'm not here because I suspect you of any crime," Murphy said. "I just want to ask you about the quality of this work and if you've seen it before."

Murphy removed a counterfeit twenty-dollar note from his wallet and placed it in Logan's hands. Logan held the bill close to his eyes and inspected both sides.

"When they told me I had TB and let me out, the first two years weren't as bad as you see me right now," Logan said. "I sought out Doc Holliday and spent some time with him in seventy-nine in Dodge City. We both have the same illness, you see. He coped with whiskey and laudanum to get him through the night. Why I'm telling you this is because when I left Dodge and traveled west to Arizona, I stopped over at Denver for a few weeks to do . . . well, let's just say for one final good time."

"Denver's a good place to do that," Murphy said.

"See that trunk beside the bed against the wall?" Logan said. "Open it and hand me the canvas sack inside."

Murphy opened the trunk and found the small canvas sack that weighed several pounds. He set it on the bed beside Logan.

"One night I got real lucky at the Metropole and won three-hundred dollars at the roulette wheel," Logan said. "Paid in twenty-dollar gold pieces."

He opened the drawstring on the sack and dumped fifteen gold coins on the bed.

"All counterfeit," Logan said.

Murphy picked up a coin. It was the right weight and circumference of a twenty-dollar gold piece.

"Lead dipped in gold," Logan said. "Now look at the workmanship."

Murphy held up the coin and examined the craftsmanship. The liberty head and thirteen stars were perfectly designed and pressed into the gold plating. The eagle and engravings on the back of the coin were equally as perfect.

"Even in my condition I can spot the work was done by the same man who made those bills," Logan said.

Murphy removed the magnifying glass from his inside jacket pocket and inspected a coin and the twenty-dollar note side-by-side.

"I will have to agree with you," Murphy said.

"I kept them as a keepsake," Logan said.

"May I have one?"

"Take them all," Logan said. "I have very little use for anything these days except for maybe a healthy pair of lungs."

Murphy nodded. "Is there anything I can do for you before I go?"

"You can take my pillow and smother me to spare me that horrible, wretched death I mentioned," Logan said.

"I'm afraid I can't do that," Murphy said.

"You would if I were a horse or your pet dog."

"That is true if you were a horse or a dog," Murphy said. "And if I remember, I'll send you a hemlock plant to brighten up your bedroom area."

"Hemlock plant?" Logan said. "Do I look like I'm in the position to care for a plant?"

Murphy gathered up the coins into the sack and tucked it into a pocket.

"And one thing you should never do is eat the leaves of a hemlock plant," Murphy said. "Eight leaves from a hemlock would kill an elephant almost on the spot."

Logan stared at Murphy.

Murphy snapped his fingers.

"Quick, like that," Murphy said. "So be sure not to eat those leaves."

Murphy nodded to Logan and stepped past the curtains.

Murphy found Sheriff J.J. Harris eating a steak supper in the restaurant at the Phoenix Hotel.

"My name is Murphy," Murphy said showing Harris his identification as he took the chair opposite the sheriff.

Harris, a large man with a big stomach and walrus mustache, looked at the identification and then at Murphy.

"What can I do for you?" he said.

"I need to send a telegram," Murphy said. "As soon as you finish your steak."

CHAPTER FIFTEEN

Murphy sat on the front porch of the Denver Hotel, and smoked his pipe and sipped coffee from a hotel dining room cup. The sun was high in the sky well past noon. The train was late. He would know when it arrived by its loud whistle.

Marshal Poule walked along the wood sidewalk and took the stairs to the porch.

"I heard you were back in town," Poule said.

"Got in last night after ten," Murphy said. "I'm waiting on a man from Washington. I figured I'd look you up when he arrives."

"About the counterfeit money?"

Murphy nodded and pulled a twenty-dollar piece from his vest pocket and flipped it to Poule.

"Counterfeit coin?" Poule said.

"I have fourteen more of them in my room," Murphy said.

"They came from Denver?"

"Metropole casino."

Poule sat in the chair to Murphy's left.

A waitress from the dining room appeared with a coffee pot and extra cup.

"Coffee, Marshal?" she asked.

"Yes, thank you," Poule said.

She filled the cup, touched up Murphy's, and disappeared back inside.

"Your man on the noon train?" Poule said. "It's late."

"The Metropole isn't going anywhere," Murphy said. "I figure when my man arrives we'll have some lunch first before walking over to the Metropole."

Burke wrestled with his conscience the entire three-day trip to Denver. On one side he felt almost a sense of duty to inform Murphy of what happened to Sally at the hands of Christopher.

On the other side, he gave Sally his word he would keep silent.

In the middle was a selfish reason best kept to himself. If Murphy knew what Christopher had done, Murphy would surely kill the man, and as bad as violating a woman was, it wasn't murder.

Murder was a hanging offense and replacing Murphy in the ranks would be no easy task for sure.

The train slowed a bit and Burke looked out the window.

Denver loomed in the background.

Burke carefully inspected the twenty-dollar gold piece and said, "The same person, are you sure?"

Murphy sliced into his steak and nodded. "Did you think I asked you to come all this way just to have lunch? I wanted you to see for yourself and take them back to the mint in Washington for closer inspection."

"And you're sure it's the same person?"

"I checked every detail under a magnifying glass," he said. "No doubt the artwork and engraving is from the same hand, but the mint can verify that."

"Dated 1875," Burke said.

"That doesn't mean a thing," Murphy said. "These coins could have been made anytime as a test — three days ago or even a decade ago, for all we know."

"I'm missing something here," Poule said. "A stack of twenty-dollar bills wouldn't weigh what one of those coins does. Why bother with coins when you can make bills?"

"If I had to guess it would be that the coins were a test to see if they stood up to scrutiny," Murphy said.

"Yes, of course," Burke said. "And if they

do, flood the area with bills."

"After lunch I'm headed to the Metropole," Murphy said to Burke. "Care to tag along?"

"That might be very interesting at that," Burke said.

The Metropole Saloon was enormous by eastern standards and larger than any saloon west of the Missouri River. It held six card tables, two blackjack tables, two roulette wheels, and four tables for other games of chance.

The bar was forty-feet long with a brass railing. Behind the bar a wall-to-wall mirror reflected every kind of whiskey and spirits imaginable.

Two bartenders were on duty at all times.

Six saloon girls worked the floor and served drinks.

"Quite a place," Burke remarked.

A crowd of a hundred or more was on hand as Murphy, Burke, and Poule walked to the bar.

"Afternoon, Marshal," one of the bartenders said.

"Claude around?" Poule asked.

"Office."

"Thanks."

Poule led Murphy and Burke to an office

door to the left of the bar. Poule knocked once and opened the door.

"Claude?" Poule said.

"Marshal Poule, what brings you to my office?" Claude said from behind his desk.

"Them," Poule said.

Murphy produced his identification and showed it to Claude.

"Secret Service, huh. Well, what can I do for you?" Claude said.

"You can shut down your business for the rest of the day so we can audit all cash and coin you have on hand," Murphy said.

"What? What for?" Claude asked.

Murphy took out the counterfeit gold coin and a twenty-dollar note and set them on the desk.

"Counterfeit money," Murphy said. "That coin, along with fourteen others just like it, came from your place. We'd like to see if there's more."

"Aw, damn," Claude said. "I have only two men in the count room. It will take all damn day and half the night to sort this out."

"Then we best get started," Murphy said.

"Can I have a drink first?" Claude asked.

"Sounds like a good idea," Murphy said.

Claude tossed back a shot of rye whiskey at

160

the bar and then turned to face the crowd of noisy patrons.

"May I have your attention please?" he said, loudly.

Most didn't hear him over the piano music. Claude nodded to the bartender, who left the bar and quieted the piano player.

"May I have everyone's attention please?" Claude said.

Slowly the crowd fell quiet and all eyes turned to Claude.

"Due to unforeseen circumstances, I am forced to close the Metropole for the rest of the day and possibly until tomorrow morning," Claude said.

"To hell you say," a man at a card table said.

"I understand it's upsetting, but I have no . . ." Claude said.

"I'm winning big," the man said. "You'll close when I say close."

Murphy quietly left the bar and walked to the man's table.

"Who the hell are you?" the man said.

"You can walk out quietly on your own," Murphy said. "Or be thrown out on your ass. Makes no difference to me."

The man stood up and as he did so, two men at the table stood with him. All three had the hard look of professional gunmen.

"I take orders from no man," the man said.

"What's your name?" Murphy said.

"Johnny Ringo."

"The gunfighter?" Murphy said.

He nodded. His right hand inched toward the silver-handled Colt revolver worn low on his hip.

"Touch it and I'll kill you," Murphy said. "And your two friends along with you if they move."

Ringo stared at Murphy.

"Go on, touch it," Murphy said.

Ringo stared at Murphy, at the man's towering height and the custom-made Peacemaker on his hip, and at the look in his eyes.

"Come on, boys," Ringo said. "Let's take our business across the street."

His two friends gathered up their winnings.

Ringo and his two friends walked away from the table and suddenly Ringo spun around and drew his Colt and froze in place as Murphy already had his Peacemaker out, cocked, and aimed.

"If you want to live, put it away real slow and keep walking," Murphy said.

Ringo slowly replaced the Colt, turned,

and walked out of the Metropole.

"Everybody, come back tomorrow," Murphy said.

As patrons filed out, Murphy returned to the bar.

"You just made Johnny Ringo back down like a kitten with its claws pulled," Poule said.

"These big-time gunfighters are all full of crap," Murphy said.

"Ringo said he's on his way to Tombstone to join the Clanton gang," Poule said. "He's been here a week. I've had no legal reason to ask him to leave town. Maybe now he'll actually go."

Murphy turned to Claude. "Where is your count room?"

"Behind the bar."

Murphy looked at Burke. "Let's go. As long as you're here you might as well be useful."

"Go ahead," Burke said. "I think I need to change my underwear."

By eight in the evening the audit was complete. Murphy showed Claude's two count men how to detect a counterfeit coin by scratching the surface with a carpenter's nail to expose the lead underneath.

In all they found twenty-seven counterfeit

gold coins all with a face value of twenty dollars, and eleven hundred in bills and notes, all in twenty-dollar denominations.

"So I'm just out this money?" Claude said.

"That is one way of saying it," Murphy said.

"What's the other way?" Claude said.

"The gold the lead is dipped in has some value," Murphy said. "When Mr. Burke returns to Washington he will wire you what it is worth in cash."

"How much?"

"I can't say for sure, but around sixty dollars is my guess," Burke said.

Claude sighed and looked at Murphy. "Can I open now? I'd like to make up for my losses."

"Go ahead, but keep an eye out for any more counterfeit notes and coins," Murphy said. "Tell the marshal the moment you get any more and try to remember who might have passed them."

Murphy and Burke drank cups of coffee on the porch of the Denver Hotel after a supper of roasted chicken with vegetables.

Piano music played softly from the Metropole Saloon and other saloons surrounding the hotel.

Murphy smoked his pipe with his coffee.

Burke lit a cigar nearly a foot long.

"You would have killed that man, that gunfighter?" Burke said.

"Johnny Ringo," Murphy said. "Yes, had he actually tried to follow through on his threat. Him and his two friends."

"How do you know he wouldn't have killed you?" Burke asked.

"Most of these gunfighters practice their tricks, but have no real speed or accuracy," Murphy said. "They feint with their left shoulder to draw your eye and then pull their gun with their right. That spin and draw thing he did he must have practiced in front of a mirror a thousand times. It works on an amateur."

"His two friends?"

"Like I said, I would have killed all three."

Burke believed he would have done just that.

"Any leads or evidence that point to a suspect?" Burke said.

"Not so much a suspect, but a trial run," Murphy said.

"Spread it around and see if it passes a test run?" Burke said.

"So to speak," Murphy said. "The thing is we don't know how long the bills and coins have been in circulation. This test run could have been planned six months or a year ago and they're ready to flood the country with hundreds of thousands or even millions in notes and bills."

"Coin?"

"I don't think so," Murphy said. "Too heavy to transport and you'd need a great deal of lead and gold and you'd have to buy or mine the amount of gold needed for wide circulation. I think the gold coins were more a pretest, feeling out to see if they passed."

"So what's next?" Burke asked.

"I'm going to see those two retired engravers on the west coast and then, if I haven't found a suspect or at least a decent lead to one, I'll go to Tennessee for a week to see Sally and help her get settled. Did she get her dogs?"

"I had to postpone picking them up a few days to meet you," Burke said. "We'll pick them up as soon as I'm home."

"I thank you for looking after her," Murphy said. "Despite what people might think of Sally she has a warm heart and worries what folks might say about me, strange as that sounds."

"That doesn't sound strange to me at all," Burke said. "I've gotten to know her a bit and she's a very sweet woman, and a decent cook at that."

"I wrote her a letter," Murphy said.

"You'll see she gets it?"

"I'll deliver it to her personally."

"Appreciate it."

"I'm going to turn in," Burke said. "My train leaves at ten and it's a long ride back to Washington."

"Wait a second," Murphy said. He dipped into his jacket pocket and produced a folded note. "When you return to Washington, go to the botanical garden and have this plant sent to Bruce Logan at the hospital in Arizona."

Burke read the note and then looked at Murphy.

"All right," Burke said.

Burke sat in a chair in his hotel room and drank whiskey from a water glass.

Murphy would have killed that gunfighter and his two friends and thought no more of it than ordering chicken at dinner tonight.

What would he do if he knew what Christopher had done to Sally?

At least with the gunfighter it would have been a case of self-defense.

With Christopher it would be outright murder.

At all costs, Burke promised himself, he would keep Sally's secret.

Partly to save Sally the anguish that would

follow, and partly to save Christopher's worthless life, but mostly to keep Murphy from life in prison or the hangman's noose.

Burke downed his glass and poured another.

He looked at Murphy's note again and wondered why on earth a man in a tuberculosis hospital would need a hemlock plant.

Chapter Sixteen

Sally opened her eyes to bright sunshine streaming in through the bedroom windows. She stared at the ceiling for a moment and then the nausea hit her like a punch to the gut and she jumped out of bed and ran across the room to the empty washbasin bowl on the dresser.

She grabbed the bowl, fell to her knees, and vomited until her stomach was empty and she dry-heaved.

Feeling dizzy and weak she sat in the chair by the window and rolled a cigarette. The heavy smoke calmed her nerves and stomach.

Then she counted backwards and did the math.

"Oh, dear God, no," she said aloud, placed her face in her hands, and started to cry.

Murphy saw Burke off at the station and

then walked back to the hotel. Marshal Poule was seated on the porch when Murphy arrived.

"Telegram for you came this morning," Poule said. "It's sealed."

Murphy took the chair next to Poule and opened the sealed envelope. The telegram was from Sheriff Goodwin in Kansas City.

From Sheriff Goodwin Kansas City Kansas. Stop Counterfeit money in town. Stop Please respond

"Problem?" Poule asked.

Murphy slid the telegram over to Poule.

"Guess you're going to Kansas City," Poule said.

"I expect so," Murphy said.

"Noon train will get you there by morning," Poule said.

"I best go pack," Murphy said.

Poule shook Murphy's hand before Murphy boarded the train.

"See you again," Poule said.

"I expect so," Murphy said.

Murphy took a seat by a window and watched Denver roll by and slowly fade from view.

Sheriff Bart Goodwin and County Sheriff Roscoe Woodward met Murphy as he walked Boyle away from the Kansas City train station.

"You must be Woodward?" Murphy said.

"I was away on county business when you were here last," Woodward said.

"Let's get some breakfast and I'll show you what we got," Goodwin said.

They ate at the hotel dining room after Murphy took Boyle to the livery stable.

Then they walked over to Goodwin's office where he unlocked his desk and dug out a small strongbox.

"One-thousand dollars in twenty-dollar bills," Goodwin said as he opened the box.

Murphy removed the bills and fanned them.

"I haven't been gone but two weeks," he said. "Who spotted it and when?"

"Three days ago by John Scott, president of the Kansas City Bank," Goodwin said. "Five-hundred dollars. The other five hundred came from the Cattlemen's Bank."

"Send a deputy for Parker," Murphy said.

Parker examined a twenty-dollar bill from the strongbox with a magnifying glass and carefully compared it to one Murphy took from his wallet.

"Same man. Same distinct style. Same paper and ink," Parker said. "No doubt."

"That's what I thought," Murphy said. "Would you say these bills were printed around the same time as the others?"

Parker rubbed the bills and then examined the ink on his fingers and the slight smudge spot on the bills using the magnifying glass.

"I would say yes they were," Parker said.

"So would I," Murphy said. "Thank you."

"I'll be at the paper if you need me," Parker said and left the office.

Murphy sat on the edge of Goodwin's desk and stuffed his pipe and lit it off a match.

"Any strangers in town?" he said.

"Only the usual cowboys and the like," Goodwin said. "It's doubtful they had five-hundred dollars between them."

"What about Kyoto?" Murphy said.

"His train was delayed due to a fire on the tracks," Goodwin said. "He showed up the next morning with his two bodyguards and checked into the hotel. He didn't leave the hotel until the next day when he took the train for Omaha."

"Do you think he has something to do with this?" Woodward asked.

"Doubtful," Murphy said. "He was in Dodge and now here when counterfeit money was found. It's probably nothing more than a coincidence."

"But you're going to check it out anyway?" Goodwin said.

Murphy nodded. "Coincidence or not, I follow the leads and right now Kyoto is the only person I know who has been in both places where counterfeit money has turned up."

"There's a direct train to Omaha in the morning," Woodward said. "Take you there before sundown."

"I'll be on it," Murphy said.

Burke arrived in Washington at eight-thirty in the morning and checked in with his office. There was nothing pressing that required immediate attention, so he took a carriage and drove it himself to Murphy's home, anxious to give the letter to Sally.

When he arrived, Sally appeared on the porch before he even stepped down from the carriage.

"I have a letter from . . ." Burke said.

"Come inside," Sally said.

Burke followed her into the living room where four pieces of luggage were on the floor. "What is . . . ?"

"I'm leaving, Mr. Burke," Sally said. "Right away."

"What do you mean leaving?"

"I'm going away."

"For how long?"

"I won't be back."

"It's Christopher, isn't it?" Burke said. "Murphy doesn't know what's happened, and I see no reason why he should. I'll fire Christopher and . . ."

"I'm pregnant," Sally said.

Burke stared at Sally.

"Christopher's?" he said.

"Yes."

"Are you sure?"

"I can count, Mr. Burke," Sally said. "I'm sure."

Burke turned to the sofa and slowly took a seat.

"Good God," he said.

"God has had nothing to do with it," Sally said.

Burke sighed. "I understand what you must feel. When?"

"I was going to hitch up Murphy's wagon, but as long as you're here would you give me a ride to the railroad?" Sally said.

"What do I tell him?" Burke said.

"Don't tell him anything," Sally said. "I don't want him to find me. Promise me that, Mr. Burke."

Burke nodded. "I'll get your bags."

■ ■ ■ ■

Murphy sat at the small desk by the window in his hotel room. He loaded up his pipe, poured a shot of his father's whiskey into a water glass, and opened his notebooks.

He read his notes and then read them again.

He emptied the glass and tossed in another ounce. The bottle was getting low. He would see if he could purchase a new bottle in Omaha.

He sipped and read his notes one more time.

When he finished the pipe and emptied the glass a second time, he closed the notebook and went to the bed.

Kyoto was in two places where counterfeit money turned up in the past several weeks.

So what?

So why didn't he trust the man?

He was here as a dignitary representing his country and to study the cattle business and what's more, showed no suspicious behavior whatsoever.

Except to be in the same places where counterfeit money turned up.

And that in itself wasn't a crime.

He stood up and returned to the desk. He

opened the notebook and got out his folded map. Denver, Dodge City, Kansas City, Omaha had what in common?

They formed a nice circle reachable by railroad in a matter of days or even hours.

If he wanted to blanket a large area with counterfeit money quickly, what better way to do it than by use of the railroad.

East of Omaha took you to the larger, more modern and sophisticated cities where banks would be more likely to spot counterfeit currency quicker than out west. Minneapolis, Chicago, Philadelphia, New York, Boston, the most advanced cities in the nation would make it nearly impossible to move a large quantity of counterfeit money undetected.

He would stay west where the towns and banks were easier to fool and maybe go further west all the way to the coast.

What was puzzling more than anything else was why go to all the trouble to produce first-rate counterfeit money only to pass small amounts?

Even if you managed to dump a thousand dollars in every town you stopped at along the railroad routes headed west, it wouldn't add up to very much. Maybe fifty thousand before you ran out of stops or got caught.

The risk outweighed the benefits.

What was happening right now was, as he first suspected, a test run.

But for what?

To accomplish what?

It would be impossible to make a profit of any large amount passing small denominations of counterfeit bills even in so large an area as the American West.

Murphy picked up a pencil and looked at his notebook.

Test was to see if the bills and notes would pass inspection upon being used at shops, saloons, and banks. Success rate of 100%.

What is the short-term goal?

What does he hope to accomplish?

What is the ultimate goal?

Murphy set the pencil down and closed the notebook.

CHAPTER SEVENTEEN

A porter carried Sally's luggage from Burke's carriage to her sleeper car on board the train.

"Is there nothing I can say or do to change your mind?" Burke said.

"How long do you think I could keep this secret from a man like Murphy?" Sally asked. "In another month, I'll start to show. And what do you think he would do when he finds out the baby isn't his?"

Burke's response was a heavy sigh.

"He would kill him and that is different than hunting a wanted criminal or murderer," Sally said. "Isn't it?"

"Yes," Burke said, defeated. "It is."

"And they hang you for committing murder, don't they?"

"Yes, they do."

The train whistle blew and a conductor called for *all aboard.*

"I shall miss you," Sally said.

She gave Burke a warm hug and a kiss on each cheek.

"You have been very kind to me and a good friend," Sally said.

And with that she turned and got aboard the train.

Murphy stepped off the train in Omaha and immediately caught wind of the nearby stockyards. Thanks in part to the railroads building the transcontinental routes through Nebraska in 1863, Nebraska achieved statehood in 1867, just two years after the end of the war.

As he retrieved Boyle from the boxcar, Murphy glanced about for Sheriff Dan Putnam, chief law enforcement official for Omaha's twenty-thousand residents. He wasn't difficult to spot. Around five-foot six inches tall with a barrel chest and enormous gut, Putnam had a full beard and hair to his shoulders. He held a double-barreled shotgun in his right hand. His badge was pinned to a red vest.

With Putnam were two deputies that appeared younger and much fitter for the job.

Murphy held up his identification. "I'm Murphy."

"Dan Putnam, sheriff of Omaha," Putnam said. "Two of my deputies, Brown and Slate.

They're good men."

"Walk with me to my hotel," Murphy said. "And we'll have some lunch and I'll tell you why I'm here."

"This is fake money?" Brown said as he inspected a twenty-dollar note.

"It's called counterfeit," Putnam said. "And I saw a fair amount of it after the war. None recently, though."

"Let me see that," Slate said.

Brown passed the bill to Slate.

"Where did this come from?" Putnam said.

"That bill came from Dodge City," Murphy said.

"Look at my hands," Slate said. "The ink."

"The natural oil on your skin causes the ink to run," Murphy said.

Slate looked at his fingers. "What oil?"

"Never mind that right now, Deputy," Putnam said. "Exactly what are you asking, Mr. Murphy?"

"How many banks in Omaha?" Murphy said.

"Six," Putnam said. "The largest being the First National Bank of Omaha."

"There are too many stores, shops, and saloons in town to audit them, but sooner or later, all cash in town passes through the banks," Murphy said. "I need all banks audited for counterfeit money, cash, and coin."

"Good God, man, that will take days," Putnam said.

"Two days at most and it can't be helped," Murphy said. "I'll visit each bank after lunch and I'd appreciate it if you went with me."

"Anything else?" Putnam asked.

"A Japanese man named Kyoto traveled through Omaha," Murphy said. "Has two bodyguards and a servant named Ito. Did you see them around town? They were here to study farming methods of corn for cattle to take back to Japan."

"I saw them," Putnam said. "They stayed at the same hotel you reserved a room at. Can't say I had much to do with them. They spent most of their time with the Grange and the Cattlemen's Association."

"When did they leave?" Murphy asked.

"Two days ago," Putnam said.

"What train did they take?" Murphy asked.

"They didn't take a train," Putnam said. "They left in a fancy coach wagon they picked up at Brogan's Livery."

"Which way did they go?" Murphy asked.

"Northwest out of town."

A waitress came to the table with a pot of coffee.

"Sorry about the wait, Sheriff," she said. "One of the girls is out with a cold."

"No problem," Putnam said. "Steaks all around and do you have some of that apple pie for dessert?"

"We do."

The waitress filled the cups and returned to the kitchen.

"Did you speak with them?" Murphy said to Putnam.

"No, but I got curious and went to see Mr. Brogan," Putnam said. "Did you ever hear of a man buying a carriage for seven-hundred dollars? That's what he paid for it and another three hundred for two horses."

"Did Brogan say if they had a conversation about where they were going?" Murphy said.

"Brogan said this Mr. Kyoto said he wanted to see some of the open west and cattle country before going home," Putnam said.

"Northwest into South Dakota might get you into the open west, but it might also get you killed by the Sioux if you go wandering around their sacred land," Murphy said.

"Do you think this Kyoto has something

to do with the counterfeit money?" Putnam asked.

"My gut says yes, the evidence says no at this point," Murphy said. "Coincidence and gut instinct do not a conviction in court make."

"We audit the banks after lunch?" Putnam asked.

"We audit the banks," Murphy said.

"You are out of your mind if you think I'm closing the bank for an entire business day so you can audit the safe," J.F. Ferguson, president of the First National Bank of Omaha, said to Murphy.

"Mr. Ferguson, I don't have the time to screw around with you on this," Murphy said. He looked at Putnam. "Post two deputies outside the bank. We'll start the audit right at closing. If we have to keep the bank closed an extra day or so and Ferguson tries to interfere, have your deputies toss him in a cell until we're done. I'll think about obstruction charges later."

"You can't do that," Ferguson said. He looked at Putnam. "Can he?"

"I believe that he can," Putnam said.

"Well damn it all to hell then, go ahead," Ferguson said.

"Keep your people as late as possible,"

Murphy said. "Maybe you won't have to lose but half a day's business tomorrow."

Brogan stood five-foot three inches tall in his boots and looked up at Murphy when Murphy walked into his office located in the rear of his very large livery business.

"What can I do for you, sir?" Brogan asked.

Murphy flashed his identification. "Tell me about the rig Mr. Kyoto purchased."

"Have you time for a drink?" Brogan asked.

"I do."

Brogan opened a bottom desk drawer and pulled out two shot glasses and a bottle of Murphy's father's whiskey.

"I first discovered this bourbon several years ago when I was purchasing wagons for a freight company in the Deep South," Brogan said. "Are you familiar with it?"

"I should be," Murphy said. "There is a very good chance that five or six years ago I bottled that batch in my father's warehouse."

Brogan filled the shot glasses. "Your father knows his trade."

"He does that, sir," Murphy said.

"Pull up a chair and tell me what you wish to know."

Murphy sat and lifted one shot glass. "To your health," he said and downed the shot.

"And yours," Brogan said and tossed back his glass.

"Mr. Kyoto of Japan purchased a carriage and two horses from you three days ago," Murphy said. "Paid for in cash."

"He did, sir," Brogan said.

"What conversations did you have with Kyoto?"

"He said he was interested in seeing some of our famous wild west before he returned to Japan," Brogan said. "He wanted a comfortable coach carriage and two horses. I had one that was ordered by a freight company in Wyoming for business use, but never picked up. I sold it and two horses for one-thousand dollars."

"In small bills no larger than a twenty?" Murphy said.

"Why, yes."

"Have you deposited them to the bank?"

Brogan thought for a moment. "I try to keep five-hundred dollars on hand for business purposes. I believe some of that money is in my safe."

"Pour another drink and let's have a look," Murphy said.

Burke sat behind his desk and waited. He

filled a water glass with whiskey, lit a cigar, and hoped that this would go well.

If it didn't, well . . .

Christopher arrived when Burke was halfway through his second drink. The cigar was down to a few inches.

"I sent for you hours ago," Burke said.

"The meeting at Congress ran late," Christopher said. "I couldn't very well leave my assignment now, could I?"

Burke sighed. "I want you to resign your position immediately," he said. "Tonight."

"Why? Because of that stupid whore?"

"She's pregnant," Burke said.

"So? It could be Murphy's or even yours for all I know," Christopher said.

"She's left Washington," Burke said. "And so should you. When Murphy learns of this, your life isn't worth a two-cent piece. I'll pay you three months' wages on top of this month's, but go you must and I mean right now."

"She was just a whore for God's sake," Christopher said.

"Now, Mr. Christopher," Burke said.

"Why you sniveling coward," Christopher said and moved toward the desk.

From his lap, Burke produced a .44 revolver, aimed it at Christopher, and cocked it. "Do I have to call the Secret Service and have you removed? There are two of them posted outside my side door."

Christopher backed off. "Three months' wages on top of this month's," he said.

With his left hand Burke slid open the top desk drawer and pulled out a thick envelope and tossed it to Christopher.

"Never return to the White House," Burke said. "And if you want to stay alive for any length of time, leave Washington."

"You're sure this money came from Kyoto?" Murphy asked.

"I'm sure," Brogan said. "I took half of Kyoto's thousand and put it in the safe to replenish my cash on hand."

"These are real," Murphy said and set four hundred in twenty-dollar bills on the desk.

Brogan looked at the pile of bills.

"These are not," Murphy said and set five, twenty-dollar notes next to the first stack.

"Counterfeit?" Brogan said.

"Pick up one of each," Murphy said.

Brogan lifted a bill from each pile and compared the two.

"It's in the paper, isn't it?" he said. "Stacked with the others one would never notice."

Murphy nodded.

"Otherwise it's perfect," Brogan said.

"As close to it," Murphy said.

"So I'm out one-hundred dollars," Brogan said.

"Unfortunately, yes."

"Could have been worse."

"Anybody else besides Kyoto and you touch these bills?" Murphy said.

"I can't speak for before he paid for the carriage, but after that I placed them into the safe where they sat until a little while ago," Brogan said. "And I'm the only one with access to my safe."

"Well, thank you for the time and the drinks," Murphy said.

On his way to the Carter Arms Hotel, Murphy stopped at a general store that was open late and purchased a dozen pencils.

In his room, Murphy filled a water glass with his father's whiskey, lit his pipe and used a small penknife to remove the wood from the pencils and then whittled the graphite shafts into a large pile of shavings on the desk.

The procedure was tedious and took awhile.

Once the last stick of graphite was shaved onto the pile, Murphy withdrew the five bills he took from Brogan and spread them out on the desk. Using thumb and forefinger, he dusted each bill with the graphite shavings until they were covered in black dust.

Then Murphy gently blew the dust off each bill to expose several different fingerprints.

From his satchel he dug out the magnifying glass and carefully studied each fingerprint. Then he removed the folded paper from his jacket pocket that had Kyoto's thumbprint on it and compared them both under the glass.

They were a match.

Two other sets of prints were on all five of the counterfeit bills. One set belonged to Brogan, Murphy was sure. The second set of prints was of thumb and forefinger and mostly smudged. The person either counted the bills or held them in such a way as to not run the ink.

On the five bills he was able to find one decent thumb and forefinger print of the third man.

"And who are you?" Murphy said aloud, and took a sip of his father's whiskey.

CHAPTER EIGHTEEN

Murphy stopped by Sheriff Putnam's office around eight in the morning and had a cup of coffee with the man.

"I'm leaving town," Murphy said. "I'd like you to oversee the audits at the banks and collect any counterfeit money and send it to Washington in care of the Secret Service in my name."

"You're going after Kyoto," Putnam said.

"I am."

"He has a three-day head start."

"In a carriage."

"What about the evidence you spoke of?"

"That's why I'm going after him," Murphy said.

Murphy picked up supplies for a week, including a full bottle of his father's whiskey from a saloon that stocked it, and rode Boyle out of town on the northwest road.

Kyoto had a three-day head start as Putnam said, but he was also traveling in a heavy carriage and wouldn't be able to make as good a time as a man alone on a good horse.

The trail was easy to follow once Omaha was in the distance. Heavy wagons and carriages make deep impressions in the earth and even heavy rain couldn't quite disguise them.

By midafternoon, Murphy had traveled ten miles and dismounted to eat a cold lunch of store-bought biscuits and jerky, and to give Boyle a few carrots and sugar cubes and a short rest.

Then he rode for another five hours and decided to make camp at a site where the wagon made camp three nights ago. A large circle of charred rocks served to protect a campfire and a place to cook on. He took advantage of it, gathered some firewood, and made a fire.

While a pot of coffee percolated and a pan of beans and bacon cooked, Murphy gave Boyle a good brushing and fed him grain and then a few carrots.

While Boyle settled down, Murphy ate and then smoked his pipe in front of the fire. Night fell silently and he spread out the bedroll and settled in for an early night.

The sky was clear and a million stars were visible.

With a little luck he could catch up to Kyoto in five days, maybe less, and if he could settle this right away, he could be home in Tennessee with Sally inside of ten days.

With a little luck.

Kyoto didn't strike Murphy as the kind of man who made careless mistakes. Everything he did was for a specific reason, even traveling by carriage when the railroad transported you where you were going much quicker.

Yet he tossed counterfeit money around Omaha almost as if he dared somebody to catch him.

And then it struck Murphy.

That was exactly what Kyoto was doing.

Daring somebody to catch the counterfeit bills as he spent them.

And no one had.

The question was why?

There was little profit, as Murphy already reasoned, in spreading small amounts of counterfeit bills in various locations around the west.

Buying the carriage was in itself a test.

And whatever test it was, in Kyoto's mind it certainly passed.

Maybe Kyoto had a much larger amount of counterfeit money or access to it than Murphy realized and he needed to test the quality before releasing it in bulk?

Why the rig?

Why suddenly buy a carriage and travel much slower than the railroad if your goal was to unload a large amount of fake money?

Murphy suddenly sat up in the bedroll.

The carriage was to transport a large quantity of counterfeit money undetected by the railroad and law enforcement in any town the railroad stopped at.

"Son of a bitch," Murphy said aloud.

Boyle, at hearing Murphy's voice, whinnied.

Murphy stood up and walked to Boyle. The massive steed was hobbled with leather strips around his legs and turned his head to nudge Murphy.

Murphy dug out a few sugar cubes from a vest pocket and fed them to Boyle.

Then he rubbed Boyle's neck and said, "We both best get some sleep now. We got a hard ride ahead of us tomorrow."

Before sunup, Murphy had coffee boiling, bacon and beans sizzling and biscuits warming, and Boyle eating grain.

They were following the carriage's trail at first light.

Around noon, when the sun was hottest, Murphy put on the dark glasses to shield his eyes from the glare and he found the trail easier to follow without having to squint.

About an hour later, the tracks veered sharply to the west. Murphy dismounted and inspected the tracks and then dug out his maps.

"Now where are they going?" he said.

He traced a path on the map.

"The Niobrara River," he said. "For access to fresh water."

Murphy mounted Boyle and rode on for another hour or so until he came upon another campsite.

"I don't know about you," Murphy said to Boyle as he dismounted. "But I'm ready for some food."

Lunch was bacon, biscuits, jerky, and coffee.

Grain for Boyle and a few sugar cubes.

Murphy studied the map while he ate.

"The Niobrara goes on for over five-hundred miles," he said to Boyle. "So Kyoto has plans for a long haul."

Close to sundown the trail took a sudden

turn to the north and Murphy kept with it until it was too dark to see the impressions in the ground made by the carriage.

While supper cooked, Murphy gave Boyle a good brushing and then fed him grain and a few sugar cubes. He ate while studying the maps by the fire.

"North," Murphy said. "To where?"

He traced several routes on the map along the Niobrara into Wyoming and north into South Dakota.

That he took a sharp turn north meant South Dakota.

But to where?

And why?

He ran his finger along the map.

"The Badlands," Murphy said, aloud.

Kyoto couldn't have been more than a day's ride ahead of Murphy when he crossed Nebraska and rode hard toward the Badlands.

He rode until noon when the Badlands were in sight.

Then he stopped and made camp.

He tended to Boyle and then made lunch and studied the maps.

The Great Sioux Nation hunted the Badlands, sometimes staying the winter if the game was good and the weather was mild.

The Badlands itself consisted of tall buttes, pinnacles, and large areas of undisturbed prairie lands. Why the hell had Kyoto chosen such a route to follow? What was his destination? Where was he transporting a large amount of counterfeit money so that he needed to risk his life on a trip through the Badlands?

A visitor to the country and a novice one at that.

You needed plenty of food and water this time of year as ninety degrees and more was normal during the day.

Murphy brushed Boyle and looked at the Badlands in the distance.

"We can make the entrance by nightfall," he said. "And in the morning I can scout around."

Murphy fed Boyle some grain and carrot sticks, then saddled him and rode until an hour before sunset. With buttes and peaks looming large just ahead of him, Murphy found a secluded spot to camp for the night.

He brushed Boyle and fed him grain and carrot sticks.

"We go in and we'll lose the wagon tracks," Murphy told Boyle. "It will become harder from there."

At dawn, Murphy sipped hot coffee and

smoked his pipe and watched the stars fade from the sky. As the sun arced, he finished his coffee and pipe and picked up the Winchester rifle from where it rested against Boyle's saddle.

He patted Boyle's neck and gave him a few sugar cubes.

"I won't be long," he reassured Boyle.

Murphy removed the binoculars from the saddlebags and looped the leather sash around his neck.

Holding the Winchester, Murphy picked out a tall peak and started to climb it. He reached the summit, around two-thousand feet high, in about an hour. The view was staggering. Buttes and peaks glowing in morning sun, open plains below shining yellow.

Off in the distance Murphy spotted a tiny object on the plains.

He used the binoculars to zoom in on the object.

It was a carriage. Abandoned. No horses in sight.

Murphy lowered the binoculars.

The son of a bitch set him up.

Kyoto knew he'd be coming for him and put the whole thing in motion to steer him in the wrong direction.

At least Murphy knew for certain that he

had the right man.

Slowly he descended the peak to the ground and put the saddle on Boyle.

Murphy dismounted Boyle a hundred feet from the carriage and took the Winchester with him when he approached it.

He opened one carriage door. Empty. Whatever Kyoto had taken with him left on horseback.

But how?

Murphy checked the two sets of tracks left by the horses. They headed east to the plains. He knelt before the tracks and they weren't deep enough the way they should be if two men and supplies rode each horse.

Kyoto left with a party of three plus his belongings and supplies.

The tracks were made by one man on each horse and weren't more than a day old.

What happened to the other two men and the supplies?

They either got off somewhere else and he missed the tracks.

Or.

They weren't in the carriage to begin with.

Murphy walked to Boyle, fed him a carrot stick, and rubbed his neck.

"What do you want to do, boy?" he said. "Backtrack all the way to Omaha, or pursue whoever left here on horseback?"

Boyle turned his head and looked at Murphy.

"Right as usual," Murphy said.

Their campfire was like a beacon to a ship at sea. They might as well be inside the lighthouse on Chesapeake Bay the fire was so easy to spot at a distance and follow. Most were not aware that the light from one candle could be seen up to one mile with the human eye.

Murphy was aware and he dismounted and walked Boyle to within five-hundred feet of the campfire and then hobbled him. He gave Boyle a carrot stick and patted his neck.

Holding the Winchester, Murphy walked in the dark toward the campfire. He stopped at a hundred feet and looked at the two cowboys leaning against a tree, each eating beans from tin plates.

The fire was directly in front of them and illuminated their faces in a reddish glow. They were behind the fire facing Murphy and the fire's glare prevented them from seeing him in the dark.

Murphy took aim with the Winchester and shattered the night with a bullet that struck the tree between the two cowboys.

Before they could react, Murphy cocked the lever and shouted, "Keep eating them beans, boys. I see a hand lower than your mouth and the next shot takes out an eyeball."

The cowboys continued eating from their tin plates.

Murphy walked to the fire and stood in front of it.

"Is that hot coffee there in that pot?" he asked.

"It is," one of the cowboys said.

"Pour me a cup," Murphy said.

"Want me to toss my gun?" the cowboy said.

"Naw," Murphy said. "If you feel lucky or stupid, pull it."

The cowboy slowly stood up and filled a tin cup with hot coffee and held it out to Murphy.

Murphy took the cup. "Now sit down and finish your supper."

The cowboy sat.

"Who hired you to drive the carriage and then leave it?" Murphy said.

The cowboys looked at each other.

"I'll kill you both, eat your beans, and think nothing of it," Murphy said. "It will take me longer with you dead, but I'll find out anyway."

"Are you law?" a cowboy asked.

"No, I'm out here in the dark for the nice climate," Murphy said.

"We're not outlaws," the other cowboy said.

"That's for sure," Murphy said. "No outlaw would leave a fire burning like that after dark. Tell me about the carriage and I won't ask again."

"We're cowpunchers," a cowboy said. "We're between jobs. This Chinaman asks us if we'd drive this wagon for him for three-hundred dollars in gold. He said he was being chased by a lawman for something he didn't do and wanted to throw him off the trail. We had nothing else to do and took the job. Three hundred is a year's pay punching cows."

"Did he tell you where to ditch the carriage?" Murphy asked.

The cowboy shook his head. "He said to head for the Badlands and leave it after five days or so and that's what we did."

"Do you know where they went?" Murphy said.

"No, but the Chinaman and his little servant got off about a mile out of town and walked to the east," the other cowboy said. "And that's the last we seen of them."

"Let me see the gold," Murphy said.

The cowboys didn't move.

"I'm not going to rob you," Murphy said. "Just show me one coin."

A cowboy pulled a small bag with a drawstring and removed a gold coin.

"Flip it here," Murphy said.

The cowboy tossed the coin to Murphy. He didn't need to examine it closely to know the coin was counterfeit and he flipped it back to the cowboy.

"You fellows have been had," Murphy said. "That money is fake."

"What are you talking about, this here is gold," the cowboy said.

"That's right it is," Murphy said. "A small amount covering a lead coin. Go on and scratch it with your knife."

The cowboy slid out his knife and scratched the surface of the coin.

"Lead," he said. "Ain't nothing but lead."

"We did all this for nothing," the other cowboy said.

"Give me the coins and I'll exchange them for real money," Murphy said. "Then you boys drive that carriage to the nearest big town and sell it. That should fetch you another three-hundred cash money."

The two cowboys looked at each other.

"What kind of lawman are you anyway?" one of them said.

"The kind that needs evidence," Murphy said. "When they got off and walked east, was anybody waiting for them?"

"Two men on horseback with two horses waiting," a cowboy said.

Murphy leaned the Winchester against his leg, dug out his wallet, and counted out six-hundred dollars in bills.

"Toss me the coins," he said.

The cowboys tossed the sacks of coins to Murphy.

Murphy set the six hundred in bills on the ground.

"Do you have a watch?" he asked.

"I do," one of the cowboys said.

"Time five minutes and then pick up your money," Murphy said. "Move before that and I'll kill you both. Now sit there against that tree and wait five minutes."

The cowboys sat back against the tree.

"And they're Japanese, not Chinamen," Murphy said.

Murphy backed up into the darkness, turned, and walked back to Boyle.

Five wasted days and nights.

Kyoto went east, but then he could have switched direction and gone anywhere.

South.

West.

North.

Anywhere at all.

Murphy dismounted about a mile from Omaha and picked up the footprints left by Kyoto and Ito as they walked east to where the two bodyguards waited on horseback. The four sets of prints turned back to Omaha.

Murphy followed the four sets of tracks directly to the railroad depot at the edge of Omaha.

Murphy tied Boyle to a post and entered the ticket office.

The man behind the counter looked at Murphy as he walked to the counter.

"Four Japanese men took a train from here ten days ago," Murphy said. "Where did they go?"

"I'm sorry, sir, but railroad policy is not to give out . . ." the man said.

"New company policy," Murphy said. "Answer my questions or I will become very, very angry with you."

The man stared at Murphy and realized he was looking at the front end of a coiled rattler. He sighed and nodded his head.

"Now where did they go?" Murphy asked.

"Santa Fe," the man said.

"Are you sure?"

"How many Japanese people do you think

are in these parts, buying train tickets?"

"When is the next train for Santa Fe?" Murphy asked.

"There is no direct route," the man said. "The next train to Topeka leaves at six this evening. From there you connect to Denver and then south to Santa Fe."

The clock behind the counter read two in the afternoon.

"How much for the ticket?" Murphy asked.

Putnam was behind his desk when Murphy barged into the office and slammed the door.

"I didn't expect to see you back in these . . ." Putnam said.

Murphy grabbed the rotund sheriff by the front of his shirt and yanked him up and over the desk and tossed him to the floor.

From a back room, Deputy Slate came running into the office.

"If you want to die this fine afternoon, move a muscle," Murphy said to Slate.

Putnam, bleeding from the nose and mouth, looked up at Murphy.

"Are you crazy?" he said. "I'm an officer of the law, same as you."

Murphy grabbed Putnam and pulled him to his feet.

"How much did he pay you to set me up?" Murphy said and slapped Putnam across the face.

Blood and spit flew from Putnam's mouth.

"How much?" Murphy asked.

"Slate, arrest this man," Putnam said as he spat blood.

Murphy slapped Putnam several more times and then flung him against the desk where Putnam slowly sank to his knees.

Murphy drew the Peacemaker and cocked it.

"Last time," Murphy said. "How much?"

Murphy stuck the Peacemaker against Putnam's skull.

Putnam collapsed to the floor.

"Five-thousand dollars," he said. "And if it makes you feel any better, after you left I tested the bills like we did at the bank and they're fake."

Murphy de-cocked the Peacemaker and holstered it. "It doesn't."

Murphy turned to Slate.

"Deputy Slate, arrest Sheriff Putnam and toss him in a cell," Murphy said.

Slate stared at Murphy.

"Move," Murphy said with such authority in his voice that Slate jumped at the command.

■ ■ ■ ■

Murphy stood in the jail cell and looked at Putnam, who sat on the bunk and held a wet facecloth to his lips.

Behind Murphy, Deputy Slate and Deputy Brown stood silently and watched.

"I'm fifty-six years old and the next election is in five months," Putnam said. "No one wants a fat, old sheriff anymore."

"Kyoto approached you with the bribe?" Murphy said.

"Yes," Putnam said. "And I took it. Five-thousand dollars is more money than I've made in the last five years. And no one got hurt. All he asked was I steer you in the wrong direction so he could put some distance between you."

"Did he say where his final destination was?" Murphy asked.

"No, and I didn't ask."

"Did Brogan know about this?"

"If he did I'm unaware of it," Putnam said.

Murphy turned to the deputies.

"Who is the senior man?" he said.

"I am by seven months," Brown said.

"You're sheriff until the next election," Murphy said.

"Can you do that?" Brown asked.

"Federal authority says that I can," Murphy said. "Do a good job and run for the office yourself."

Murphy sat by the window in a riding car and watched the train slowly leave the station. It would be morning by the time he reached Topeka where he would catch the next train to Denver and then south to Santa Fe.

Murphy opened his notebook and let his thoughts run freely on paper.

Why all the running around?
Kyoto knew Murphy was after him and created the diversion to buy some time.
But time to do what?
To go where?
He must have some larger goal than spreading small amounts of counterfeit money across the west.
Some higher purpose.
What was in Santa Fe?

Murphy gazed out the window at the rolling scenery for a moment.

Santa Fe was a cattle town, but it was obvious at this point that Kyoto had no interest in cattle. Counterfeit money was his game and up to this point he'd been making test runs.

So what does he do now?

Empty his vault and dump a large amount of counterfeit money on the great southwest?

For what purpose?

What was his gain in such an act?

Murphy stared straight ahead as he thought.

Santa Fe was not a major metropolis by any stretch of the imagination. It was a cowboy town with limited potential for a man like Kyoto.

Except for one thing.

The railroad to the west coast where a four-mast schooner to Japan awaited.

Murphy looked out the window.

"The son of a bitch is going home," he said aloud.

The town of Topeka was dead asleep when the train arrived at two in the morning. Murphy was the only passenger to get off and the conductor, in a hurry to get rolling again, almost took off before Murphy could retrieve Boyle from the boxcar.

Murphy walked Boyle down Main Street and tied him to a post outside the sheriff's office. Light from a lantern shone through the plate-glass window to the street. He could see a man sleeping at a desk.

Murphy opened the door, stepped inside, and then slammed the door closed.

The man all but fell over backwards in his chair.

"The good people of Topeka pay you to sleep the night away?" Murphy asked.

"Who the hell are you?" the man said.

Murphy looked at the deputy badge pinned to the man's vest.

"I'm Deputy Sheriff McCall."

Murphy pulled his wallet and tossed it on the desk. McCall opened it and read the identification.

"I've heard of you," McCall said.

"Where's the sheriff?"

"Asleep at his home."

"Go wake him," Murphy said. "I'll wait."

McCall stared at Murphy.

"I wasn't asking," Murphy said.

Thirty minutes passed before McCall returned with Sheriff Coffey.

Murphy was drinking coffee in a tin cup from the pot kept warm on the woodstove. He was seated at the desk and had lit his pipe.

"Is that my cup you're drinking from?"

Coffey said.

"Probably," Murphy said.

"Now that you got me out of bed, what do you want?" Coffey demanded.

"A party of four Japanese men came through here nine days ago and caught a train west to Denver," Murphy said. "Do you remember them in town?"

"I do," Coffey said. "But they had to wait around for several days to catch a train to Denver."

Murphy sat up straight in the chair. "Why?"

"Where have you been the last week?" Coffey said. "Some Apache war chief has been running around burning railroad tracks all over the place."

"Burning tracks?" Murphy said.

"He's got a burr up his ass over the government canceling some contract to build some sort of Indian hospital," Coffey said.

"What happened to the four Japanese?"

"They waited around two days and then caught the next train to Denver," Coffey said. "But I got word the tracks were burned and the train was abandoned."

"Abandoned where?" Murphy asked.

"How the hell do I know?" Coffey said. "Somewhere between here and Denver."

"That's close to five-hundred miles of track," Murphy said.

"It is," Coffey said as he picked up a tin cup off the mantel above the woodstove and filled it with coffee. "And now if you don't mind, what is this all about?"

"Those men are wanted for federal crimes," Murphy said.

"That's why you and not a sheriff's posse?"

Murphy nodded. "The tracks repaired?"

"Every time one section is fixed they burn another," Coffey said. "Who knows?"

"Where's the telegraph office?" Murphy said.

"It's almost three in the morning," Coffey said.

"I know what time it is," Murphy said. "Get the operator out of bed and open the damned office."

Coffey nodded to McCall.

"Get him out of bed," Coffey said.

"What the hell do you mean I can't come in?" the telegraph operator said. "It's my damn office."

"And you can have it back just as soon as I'm through," Murphy said and shut the door and locked it.

Murphy struck a match and lit the oil

lantern on the desk.

He held his finger over the telegraph key for a moment as he composed a message in his mind.

Then he tapped in his private code directly to Burke at the White House.

To William Burke Stop From Murphy Stop. Apache War Chief Ten Moons burning railroad tracks on southwestern routes Stop Alert Army and US Marshals to not pursue Stop Repeat Do not pursue Apache Ten Moons Stop Counterfeiters stalled due to track repair Stop Murphy in pursuit Stop Will telegraph again when arrive in Denver Stop Murphy

Murphy thought for a moment and then sent a second telegram.

To US Marshal Poule Denver Stop From US Secret Service Agent Murphy. Stop Ten Moons Apache War Chief burning railroad tracks from Topeka to Denver. Stop Do not pursue Ten Moons Stop Repeat Do Not Pursue Ten Moons Stop Will explain when I arrive in Denver Stop Murphy.

He sat for a moment and pulled out his

pipe, filled it, and lit a match. Then he went outside where Coffey, McCall, and the telegraph operator were waiting.

"Sheriff, the train that I arrived on is still at the station," Murphy said.

"I saw the conductor and engineer at the hotel a few minutes ago," McCall said. "They said they're under orders from the railroad to stay put due to the track burnings."

"Get them," Murphy said. "Wake the hotel manager and have them open the restaurant. We'll meet there in fifteen minutes."

McCall stared at Murphy.

Murphy sucked on his pipe.

"I know," McCall said. "You weren't asking."

Engineer Hub Jackson and conductor Jep Tyler were hard, career railroad men. A team since sixty-seven, they covered more than a half-million miles together and survived Indian raids, robberies from outlaws, mudslides, fire, derailments, and even an earthquake, but never had they heard of anything like what Murphy was suggesting.

"Let me see if I understand you properly," Tyler said. "You want my engineer to run two cars all night west to Denver against

214

orders from the railroad that halted all scheduled trains due to Apaches burning track? Is that what you're asking?"

A sleepy waitress approached the table with a tray of cups and a pot of coffee. She set a cup in front of Murphy, Coffey, McCall, Tyler, and Jackson and filled them with hot coffee.

"Eggs, bacon, biscuits, and juice in about fifteen minutes," she said and returned to the kitchen.

"Do you have a problem with taking a direct order from a federal authority that supersedes the railroad?" Murphy said. "Because if you do, I will commandeer the train and drive it myself."

Tyler looked at Jackson and the two men grinned.

"Hell, mister, we've been waiting for the chance to bust loose for years," Tyler said.

"How soon can you be ready?" Murphy said.

"Right after breakfast," Tyler said.

"What's commandeer mean?" McCall said.

Coffey and McCall stood on the platform with Murphy and Boyle as Tyler and Jackson readied three railroad cars.

Tyler walked to Murphy.

"We're taking on enough water, coal, and wood to make three-hundred miles," he said. "We'll make one stop to resupply and then get as close to Denver as possible. Go ahead and box your horse. We'll be off inside o' ten minutes."

The waitress from the hotel restaurant walked onto the platform with a pot of coffee and a paper sack. "Two dozen biscuits for the ride," she said.

"Thank you kindly," Tyler said.

From inside the locomotive, Jackson said, "Ready when you are."

Murphy boxed Boyle and then climbed aboard the locomotive with Tyler and Jackson.

Coffey, McCall, and the waitress watched as the three-car train slowly pulled away from the station and rode off into the night.

"Damndest thing I ever saw," Coffey said.

McCall looked at the waitress.

"Any more of those biscuits?" he asked.

CHAPTER NINETEEN

A few miles west of Topeka, Murphy filled a tin cup with hot coffee and watched the gauges. They were traveling at the speed of forty miles per hour, the speed of the fastest horse.

"Can we go fifty?" Murphy said.

"She's just getting warmed up," Jackson said. "Give her a bit and she'll top fifty."

Tyler filled a tin mug with coffee and stood beside Murphy. As Tyler sipped, a bit of coffee spilled down his shirt.

"I wish the hell some company back east would invent a coffee cup with a lid on it," Tyler said.

"A lid?" Jackson said. "That would never catch on."

Tyler read the gauges.

"Take her to fifty," he said.

Grinning, Jackson worked the handles and the needle slowly moved to fifty.

"Son of a bitch it feels good to bust loose,"

217

Jackson said.

Tyler sat in the conductor's chair beside Jackson.

Murphy stood beside the open window and sipped his coffee. The horizon was starting to lighten and sunrise would follow soon.

"All this power and speed in my hand, an open track, and riding into the sunrise, what could be better than that?" Jackson said.

Shirtless, Murphy shoveled coal into the furnace until they glowed red and then he slammed the door shut.

"How far have we come?" he asked.

"Closing in on two-hundred miles," Jackson said.

"When will we have to stop for water and coal?"

"Got a stop the next fifty miles," Tyler said. "If we need to we can burn wood if the coal is low."

"How soon do you slow down before you reach the stop?" Murphy said.

"I start slowing her a good five miles out a little at a time so I can stop her on a dime," Jackson said.

"Start slowing speed ten miles out and wake me," Murphy said as he slipped into his shirt, sat against the wall, and lowered his hat over his eyes.

Murphy opened his eyes when Tyler gently nudged him.

Instantly Murphy was awake.

Tyler handed him a cup of coffee.

Murphy stood and looked out the window. They were traveling at ten miles per hour. "How far to the water stop?" he asked.

"Two and a half, maybe three miles," Jackson said.

Murphy looked to the hills on the right.

"Do you see that?"

"Why do you think I'm slowing down?" Jackson said.

Murphy dug his binoculars out of his satchel and scanned the hills and locked in on the Apache warrior on horseback who was watching them with more than a keen interest. In full dress and war colors, Winchester rifle in hand, the Apache was an imposing sight.

"Stop the train," Murphy said.

"We're not close enough to the . . ." Tyler said.

"Now. Right here," Murphy said.

Tyler looked at Jackson.

"Do it," Tyler said.

Jackson slowed the train to a stop.

"Wait for me to clear the train and then

move out," Murphy said. "I'll meet you at the water stop later on."

"That's an Apache out there," Tyler said. "Where there's one, there's more."

"Have I suddenly become inarticulate?" Murphy asked.

Tyler sighed. "We'll wait for you at the water stop."

Murphy jumped down to the ground and walked to the boxcar and slid open the door.

Boyle looked at him.

Murphy climbed into the boxcar and picked up the saddle.

"Let's run off some of the fine grain you've been eating," Murphy said.

Five minutes later, Murphy jumped Boyle out of the boxcar to the ground and broke him into a flat-out run toward the Apache on the hill.

As Murphy neared the hill, the Apache didn't move and a second Apache on horseback appeared by his side.

Even from a distance of five-hundred feet Murphy recognized the second Apache as the ever-imposing figure of Ten Moons.

Murphy rode up the hill and stopped directly in front of Ten Moons.

Ten Moons, stone-faced, glared at Murphy.

"I figured you'd be fat and happy with

your woman by now," Ten Moons said.

"Nothing would suit me finer," Murphy said. "But I have to finish a job first before that can happen."

"Want some lunch?" Ten Moons said.

"What's on the spit?"

"Rabbit."

"I'll take you up on that," Murphy said.

"Have you coffee?" Ten Moons said.

"I do."

"Sugar?"

"I do."

"That fine whiskey your father makes?"

Murphy grinned. "Let's go."

Ten Moons, Murphy, and two-dozen Apache warriors sat in a circle around a large spit. Several rabbits roasted on sticks. Murphy's coffee pot boiled on the open fire. He filled two tin cups with coffee, added sugar and a splash of his father's whiskey, and handed one cup to Ten Moons.

Ten Moons took a sip.

Murphy grinned. "Why don't you carry coffee and a pot in your supplies?"

"It wouldn't be Apache," Ten Moons said.

"It wouldn't be Apache to drink it, either, but that doesn't stop you," Murphy said.

"An Apache doesn't insult a guest by refusing his gift."

"Gift?" Murphy grinned. "Hell, you asked me for it."

Both men sipped their coffee.

Murphy stuffed his pipe and lit it with a match.

"Tell me about the railroad burnings," Murphy said.

Ten Moons took another sip from his cup, and then said, "The hospital my son was building, the man from Indian Affairs stopped it."

"Why?"

"He said my son stole the money and that my son would have to face the white man's court of law."

"They have some truly stupid people at Indian Affairs," Murphy said. "I'll put a stop to that right away. In fact, I'll have the president personally send a letter of apology and double the amount I gave your son."

Ten Moons looked at Murphy. "You have that much power?"

"I know where the skeletons in Washington are buried," Murphy said. "You have my word things will be made right inside a month."

"So you didn't come here to stop me?" Ten Moons said.

"Hell, I don't care if you burn every track

from New York to San Francisco," Murphy said.

"I'm confused," Ten Moons said.

"There are four men that I'm after," Murphy explained. "They are very dangerous to the country. They were on the train to Denver when you burned the tracks and they had to get off. How far from Denver did you set the fire?"

"An hour's ride past the big water tank," Ten Moons said.

"Did you stick around to watch?"

"Of course," Ten Moons said. "What fun would there be in leaving?"

"The four men I'm after are foreigners," Murphy said. "From the country of Japan. Dark hair and skin with eyes different than a white man. Did you see such men get off the train?"

"Everybody got off the train," Ten Moons said. "But the four men you want are the only four who did not get back on."

"Where did they go?"

"South on foot."

Murphy stood up and went to dig out his maps from the saddlebags and then returned to sit next to Ten Moons.

With his finger, Murphy traced a path. "That would be here," he said.

Ten Moons looked at the map.

"And they went south on foot," Murphy said.

Murphy ran his finger south and slightly east to the tiny town of Gatesville.

"To here," Murphy said. "Gatesville."

"I know that town," Ten Moons said. "There is nothing there but tumbleweed and dust."

"There is one thing there they need," Murphy said. "Horses."

Ten Moons nodded.

Murphy ran his finger south on the map.

"To ride to Santa Fe to catch the railroad west to California," he said.

Ten Moons looked at the map.

"If they have repaired the many miles of track we burned between Colorado Springs and Santa Fe by now," he said.

Murphy shook his head and grinned. "How did the Army not catch up to you?"

"The Army," Ten Moons said with disgust. "They couldn't track a pregnant doe in the snow if it wore a cow bell."

"Let's have some more coffee," Murphy said.

"Sweeten mine a bit more," Ten Moons said.

Tyler and Jackson waited in the locomotive for Murphy. They were nervous and jittery and weren't sure if Murphy would return or not.

"Two hours," Tyler said.

Then they saw it and couldn't believe it even though they were looking right at it. Murphy and Apache Ten Moons riding side-by-side with two-dozen warriors behind them in two columns.

Murphy and Ten Moons rode to within a few feet of the locomotive.

"Jackson, Tyler, this is my old friend Ten Moons," Murphy said.

Jackson and Tyler stared at the Apache chief.

"You were right," Ten Moons said. "They aren't worth killing."

Jackson and Tyler looked at Murphy.

Ten Moons winked at Murphy, then turned his horse and quickly rode away with his braves directly behind him.

"Fire her up, gentlemen, while I put my horse away," Murphy said.

About an hour later, Jackson slowed the train to a stop fifty yards from the burned-out track.

"At least another hundred and fifty or more miles to Denver," Tyler said.

"You men head on back," Murphy said.

"You're getting off?" Tyler said.

"I am," Murphy said.

He jumped down and walked back to retrieve Boyle and then rode to the locomotive.

"Tell Coffey I went south to Gatesville after Kyoto," Murphy said. "Tell him to send a wire to all marshals from here to the Mexican border to keep an eye out for them."

"Good luck," Tyler said.

Murphy rode Boyle across the tracks and south and looked for signs of Kyoto and his men. They weren't difficult to spot in the dry sand and dirt near the tracks. Kyoto in the lead, followed closely by his two bodyguards and then Kyoto's manservant.

"Let's go, boy," Murphy said.

It was close to sundown when Murphy arrived at the fringe of Gatesville. The town consisted of twenty-five or so buildings on three streets. The town served as a way station for freight shipped by wagon to areas not covered by the railroad.

Ten of the buildings were actually small warehouses. A large livery stable with a dozen or more freight wagons lined the first of the three streets. The second street had a saloon, general store, freight offices, gunsmith, a small jailhouse, and a blacksmith shop.

The third street had a dozen, two-story homes where residents of the town lived.

Bleak was the word that came to mind as Murphy rode past the warehouses to the second street.

Light from the saloon illuminated the street as he turned down the second street and dismounted in front of the dreary-looking watering hole.

Murphy wrapped Boyle's reins around the post and then slipped the Winchester from its sleeve to take into the saloon with him.

The street was void of pedestrians and why not, there wasn't a damn thing to do in Gatesville after dark except drink and line up for the girls on the second floor above the saloon.

As Murphy stepped up onto the wood sidewalk a shot rang out as a bullet whizzed by his hat and took out the saloon window.

Murphy tossed his body onto the wood sidewalk and rolled off it to the dirt street behind a water trough. Boyle, a few feet away, looked down at him.

"I know, boy," Murphy said.

He reached up with the Winchester and loosened Boyle's reins and a second shot rang out and a hole appeared above the water line in the trough.

"Wait for me down the street," Murphy said. "Go."

Boyle looked at Murphy.

"Go," Murphy said.

Boyle trotted twenty feet down the street, stopped, and looked back at Murphy.

Murphy scanned the buildings across the street. They were dark and with the sun down now it was impossible to see who was shooting.

Question was why?

He'd been in town all of five minutes and hadn't even spoken to anyone yet.

The lanterns inside the saloon went out, but the oil lantern hung outside above the door was still lit.

Murphy took aim with the Winchester and fired a shot at the lantern and it exploded into a dozen pieces that tossed oil and fire onto the wall of the saloon and wood sidewalk.

Within seconds the wall and sidewalk were on fire.

Murphy rolled away into the dark and then tucked himself under the overhang of the sidewalk.

As the flames grew higher, men inside the saloon rushed out and jumped down to the street.

"Son of a bitch," a man shouted.

"Get buckets, quick," another shouted.

As the men raced for buckets and filled them from the trough, Murphy scanned the buildings across the street and saw a man with a rifle on a rooftop.

Murphy cocked the lever of the Winchester and took careful aim and gently squeezed the trigger.

The bullet struck the man in the head and he fell backward as if chopped down with an ax.

The crowd on the street froze and turned to look at Murphy as he slowly stood up from the shadows. Light from the flames danced off his face and made his eyes appear yellow and sinister.

"What the hell are you looking at me for?" Murphy said, as he grabbed an empty water bucket. "Put that fire out."

With the acrid smell of smoke lingering inside the saloon, Murphy took a small sip of whiskey from a shot glass and looked at the crowd of thirty or so men standing before him. On the stairs to his right, six women from the second-floor brothel watched him with keen interest.

"Who is in charge of this Godforsaken place?" Murphy said, as he held up his identification for all to see.

A short, stout man stepped forward from the crowd.

"That be me," he said. "Name is Henshaw."

"Well, Mr. Henshaw, why did that man shoot at me from the roof?" Murphy asked.

Henshaw had a shot glass in his right hand and downed the whiskey and then walked to the bar and stood beside Murphy.

Murphy lifted a bottle of rye off the bar and filled Henshaw's shot glass.

"Obliged," Henshaw said and lifted the glass. "Four foreigners walked into town five days ago," he said and sipped. "They said the train was burned out and they walked from the point where they got off. They said a man was after them and they would pay one thousand in gold to anybody who stopped him. They never said the man was a government agent."

"They offered gold?" Murphy asked.

"They wanted to buy four horses with saddles, but we can't spare any on account of all the freight," Henshaw said. "That idiot who shot at you was William Blue, but folks just call him Billy or Blue. He owns a small horse ranch a few miles west of here and happened to be in town getting his bean wiggled when the foreigners came through.

He sold them four horses and took the thousand in gold. We didn't think him serious, but I guess that he was."

"And how long ago did the bean wiggler sell them the horses?" Murphy said.

On the stairs, the women giggled.

"You women hush," Henshaw said. "Four days ago Billy rode in with the horses and they left around noon or so."

"South?"

"That's where they headed."

Murphy tossed back his shot of rye. "I'll pay for the casket to bury Mr. Blue," he said.

"No need," Henshaw said. "We found the thousand in gold coin still on him when they took him down from the rooftop."

Murphy grinned slightly. "Suit yourself," he said. "Is there a place I can rent a room for tonight?"

"We got an empty room," one of the six women on the stairs said.

"That probably be the only one," Henshaw said.

Murphy removed a twenty-dollar bill from his fold and set it on the bar. "For livery of my horse," he said.

"That's a fifty-cents expense for overnight," Henshaw said.

"I know," Murphy said. "The other nineteen-fifty is to make sure nothing happens to my horse."

"He'll be fine," Henshaw said. "My word on it."

"I'll take that at face value," Murphy said. "But if you break your word they will be building two coffins in the morning."

Murphy turned to the women on the stairs.

"Ladies," he said and picked up his saddlebags and satchel. "Show me that room."

Sadie, the oldest of the six women at thirty-two, was in charge of the second-floor operations. She was a plump woman with a pretty face and hair so blond it appeared yellow.

"We got seven rooms up here," she said. "One for each of us to live in and a spare for any overnight stranger passing through. We also got a parlor and a full kitchen. Might you be interested in some home cooking?"

"I would," Murphy said.

"This way," Sadie said and parted a door made of beads to the kitchen where the other five women were setting plates at the table and pouring beef stew.

"Ladies, be seated," Sadie said. "Mr. Murphy, you are to my right."

Once everyone was seated, Sadie said,

"Gabby, it's your turn to say grace."

Murphy glanced around the table as the six women folded their hands and bowed their heads.

He removed his hat and set it on the floor beside his chair.

A dark-haired woman who Murphy thought might have been Mexican said, "Jesus, it's to you we pray. We are thankful for this food and for our health and for allowing Mr. Murphy not to get shot earlier tonight. Amen."

Murphy looked at Sadie.

"We're prostitutes, Mr. Murphy, not heathens," she said.

Murphy, Sadie, and the five women took after-dinner coffee and cake in the parlor.

"We do all our own cooking and baking," Sadie said. "And many a cowboy and freighter have paid more for the food than for dipping his bean in the pot."

"I can understand why," Murphy said. "The stew was excellent and this cake is wonderful."

"Thank you, Mr. Murphy," Sadie said. "And girls, speaking of bean dipping, best go to your rooms and get ready for tonight's rush. Remember to brush your teeth and don't skimp on the talc."

After Murphy and Sadie were alone, she refilled his coffee cup and sat close to him. "How about you, Mr. Murphy?" she said. "My room is vacant and very comfortable."

Murphy took a sip from his cup and then said, "There is a wonderful woman waiting for me at home and she wouldn't approve of my behavior if I took up your offer."

Sadie stared at Murphy for a moment, and then shook her head.

"First real man to come through here in years and he has to have a conscience," she said.

"I'll say goodnight and if it's possible, I'll pay the ladies for fixing me some traveling food," Murphy said. "Biscuits and corn dodgers would do nicely."

"We can do that," Sadie said. "And if you change your mind my room is right next to yours."

Alone in his room, Murphy turned the oil lantern to a high flame and studied his maps.

Kyoto had a three- or four-day head start, but if the railroad tracks were still out, he would have to ride all the way to Santa Fe and he didn't strike Murphy as an experienced horseman. Plus he didn't know the country, and that in itself would slow a man down.

With a bit of luck he could catch up to him inside of three days, four at most.

Murphy blew out the oil lamp and settled into the very comfortable bed.

He closed his eyes and fought hard to keep Sally's face out of his thoughts. When the job was over and he returned to Tennessee, he would take her on a long vacation. Maybe take a schooner to a warm island off the Florida coast and do nothing but sit in the sun and sip cold drinks, and later watch the sunset from chairs on the beach.

She would like that was his final thought before falling asleep.

CHAPTER TWENTY

After breakfast with Sadie and the ladies, Murphy was presented with two canvas sacks.

"One has one hundred and twenty-five corn dodgers in it," Sadie said. "The other has forty biscuits. My girls baked them all early this morning."

"I appreciate it," Murphy said as he dug out his billfold.

He removed five twenty-dollar bills and placed them in Sadie's hands.

"For a little flour and grease?" she said. "Why, you didn't even pay me a visit."

"For the hospitality," Murphy said. "And that's worth more."

Henshaw caught up with Murphy as he came out of the general store carrying forty pounds of supplies.

"Something you should know," Henshaw said. "Blue has two brothers and a cousin and they live on a small spread close to Blue's. They picked up the body this morning. They said after they gave Blue a proper burial they would be coming for you."

Murphy stuck the supplies into his saddlebags and pulled the straps tight.

"And you said?"

"Nothing," Henshaw said. "Those Blues are a nasty bunch. Words mean nothing to them, nothing at all. I'm not sure a one of them can even write. They're gonna do what they're gonna do and that's all there is to it."

Murphy tightened the saddle a bit on Boyle.

"A real nice town you got here," he said.

"We're not cowards," Henshaw said. "We're freighters, and we do important work in the territory. It ain't our fault we got no law out here."

Murphy mounted Boyle in one swift and graceful motion.

"Yeah, it is," he said and rode off.

It wasn't difficult to pick up Kyoto's tracks. They kept the same formation as earlier, with Kyoto in the lead, his two bodyguards behind him, and Ito bringing up the rear.

The four sets of tracks blended in with dozens of wagon tracks and other horses, but after a few miles, when the wagons veered off to the east or west, Kyoto became easier to follow.

The closest major town was Colorado Springs, about two days' ride south and to the west a bit.

It wasn't a railroad town, but it was a good place to resupply, rest up for a day, and prepare for the four- or five-day ride to Santa Fe, where the railroad connected all the way to the Pacific.

They stayed in their pecking order and rode at a steady, if not hurried pace. Kyoto thought either Murphy was dead or so far behind that he would never catch up to him before Santa Fe, Murphy reasoned.

Or.

That Murphy was no threat at all.

"Let's give Mr. Kyoto something to worry about," Murphy said and broke Boyle into a fast trot.

At twelve-thirty by his pocket watch, Murphy dismounted and tied Boyle's reins to brush under a pine tree in the shade.

He built a fire and cooked some bacon and beans in a pan and filled the coffee pot with enough water for three cups.

While he waited for lunch to cook, Murphy fed Boyle grain and brushed him thoroughly with his heavy brush.

Then Murphy sat in the shade with a plate of beans, bacon, coffee, and several of Sadie's biscuits.

Sopping up sauce from the plate, Murphy looked at Boyle. "It's the little things in life you come to appreciate the most," he said and bit into the sauce-soaked biscuit.

When lunch was done, Murphy stuffed his pipe and drank the last bit of coffee under the tree next to Boyle.

"The way I see it we can continue on and wait to get bushwhacked in our sleep," Murphy said. "Or we can stay right here until the Blue clan catches up to us. What's your opinion on the matter?"

Boyle turned his head and looked at Murphy.

"I agree," Murphy said. "The hell with the Blues."

Murphy took a sip of water and removed his dark glasses so he could pour some water onto his hand and dampen his face.

The afternoon sun was hot. He wanted another sip of water, but he knew better. In sun like this, the more you drank, the more you sweat and then you'll want more. It was best to wait until dark to quench your thirst.

He was about to stuff his pipe when he

spotted three specs on the horizon. He set the pipe aside and picked up his binoculars.

Three men on horses riding his way.

The Blue clan.

He judged the time at about two hours before they were in range.

He checked his watch. They should arrive around five o'clock.

"I should have brought the Sharps," he said aloud.

He gathered up his things and went to sit beside Boyle in the shade.

He removed his writing paper and a pencil from a saddlebag and started a new letter to Sally. He wrote three pages, occasionally glancing up to track the Blues. At the start of the fourth page, he set paper and pencil aside and stood up with the Winchester in hand.

"If something should happen," Murphy said and removed the saddle, "you head for the clearing up there and don't look back. Spend your old age with some young filly and sire a few ponies for the bloodline."

Murphy walked out to the clearing and judged the distance to the Blues at four-hundred yards.

He cupped his right hand. "That's far enough," he shouted.

It took a few seconds and then the three

Blues paused. One of them shouted back at Murphy.

"You be the man who murdered our Billy?"

"I killed him, that's for sure, but it wasn't murder," Murphy yelled. "He was shooting at me from a rooftop in the dark. I defended myself and that resulted in him getting shot. That's all there is to it."

"We know that. We don't care. No man kills ours and lives to tell about it," a Blue shouted.

Murphy shook his head and sighed softly.

"Turn back before it's too late," he shouted.

"Too late for you," a Blue shouted.

"You won't listen to reason then?" Murphy shouted.

"You go to hell," a Blue shouted.

"You first," Murphy whispered.

He aimed the Winchester at the center Blue and then slowly squeezed the trigger.

The Blue in the center flew backwards off his horse to the ground.

The remaining two Blues immediately turned their horses and rode back to widen the distance out of the Winchester's range.

Murphy cocked the lever, aimed, and dropped the Blue on the left with a shot to the head.

He quickly cocked the lever again, aimed, and fired. The remaining Blue fell off his horse and as the horse ran off the remaining Blue started to crawl.

Murphy turned and walked back to Boyle, reached for the saddle, and quickly strapped it on. In one swift motion, Murphy was in the saddle and stuck the Winchester into the sleeve, and then raced Boyle to the Blue, who was still crawling on his belly.

Murphy slid off the saddle and walked to the crawling man. The bullet from the Winchester tore a hole in the man's right lung and he was bleeding heavily.

Murphy reached down and turned the man over.

He was young, in his early twenties.

"You left me no choice," Murphy said.

"You go to hell you son of a bitch," the Blue said.

"I can stop the bleeding and save your life," Murphy said. "In exchange for your word you won't try to kill me again."

"Like I said, you go to hell," the Blue said and spat at Murphy.

Murphy took a step back and looked at the Blue.

"You don't have to die today," Murphy said. "Give me your word you won't come after me."

"Screw you," the Blue said.

"Have it your way," Murphy said. "I won't kill you. I'll let the land do that."

Murphy walked to Boyle and was about to place his foot in the stirrup when he heard the click of a pistol being cocked. In an instant, Murphy drew his Peacemaker, cocked it, spun, and fired.

The third Blue was sitting up with his cocked revolver aimed at Murphy.

The bullet struck the third Blue dead center in the heart. The revolver fell from his hand as he slumped over dead.

"Oh, Goddammit," Murphy said. "You stupid son of a bitch."

He holstered the Peacemaker and turned to Boyle.

On the right side of the saddle was a small, folding shovel and Murphy removed it. "Might as well get comfortable, boy. This is going to take awhile."

Murphy finished the final grave by the light of a campfire. Earlier, he'd set their horses free.

"I don't feel obliged to say a few words over them," he said aloud. "They belong to you now, God, and you're welcome to them."

He walked to Boyle and dug out the grain.

"Let's eat something," Murphy said.

Kyoto's tracks led directly to the town of Silver Springs. A half mile or so from the edge of the town, Murphy paused and dug out the binoculars and took a closer look from the saddle.

"Doesn't look like much of a place to me, boy," he said to Boyle. "Nonetheless, let's go in slow and easy."

Main Street was a hub of activity. Most of the three-hundred residents of Silver Springs were gathered for the results of the local election held the day before for mayor and sheriff.

Murphy dismounted and walked Boyle along Main Street to the festivities where tables were lined with fried chicken, mashed potatoes, breads, and beer. As he walked past the tables, he grabbed a chicken leg and a warm biscuit and stood behind the crowd to eat them.

A short man in a black suit was standing on a wood crate holding court. A man wearing a sheriff's badge stood to his left and another man in a gray suit stood to his right.

"Results are final," the man on the crate said. "Dan Griffith here is the new mayor and Walt Robbins is the new sheriff. Good luck to them both. The bar is now open."

The crowd let go with a loud cheer and rushed to the tables.

Finished with the chicken leg, Murphy tossed it into a waste bin constructed of wood and approached the new sheriff.

"Congratulations," Murphy said.

Robbins scanned Murphy quickly and said, "I'm not so sure about that."

"Is there a place we can talk in private?" Murphy said.

"About?"

Murphy dug his identification out of his jacket pocket and held it up for Robbins to read.

Robbins sighed.

"Let me grab a chicken leg and a beer first," he said.

The sheriff's office was a small, cramped room with space for one desk, a rack of rifles, a Franklin woodstove, and one jail cell.

"Haven't even moved in yet," Robbins said as he bit into a chicken leg.

Murphy also had a leg and a glass of beer. He set the beer on the desk and said, "Four men, foreigners on horseback, rode through here. They're Japanese. Did you see them?"

"Yeah, I saw them," Robbins said. "Passed through here three days ago. One of them was injured. Fell off his horse. They had him tied to the saddle so he wouldn't fall off again, I suppose. We ain't got a real doc, but the horse vet fixed him up a bit."

"Which one was injured?" Murphy said.

"Little man about forty or so."

"How long did they stay?"

"Overnight. They bought a wagon and left with the injured man in back."

"They went south?"

Robbins nodded. "What's this all about?"

"Those men are wanted. Where is the horse vet?"

James Hobbs lived in a yellow house with green trim at the very edge of town. His wife, Iris, kept a flower bed out front and another one out back and she served as his nurse when needed, usually when surgery was called for on a horse or mule, and the occasional pig.

Iris served tea with little shortbread cookies to Murphy and her husband in the parlor while the two men talked.

"They said that he fell off his horse," Hobbs said. "In my opinion he didn't."

"Because?" Murphy said as he sipped some of Iris's tea.

"I've seen and treated enough human injuries and wounds to know the difference

246

between a bruise made when you fall off a horse and when you're beaten," Hobbs said.

"And he was beaten?"

"To within an inch of his life."

"With fist or weapon?"

"Strange, but no fists or boots," Hobbs said. "The bruises were elongated as if he was hit with a stick. And another thing struck me as odd. His face, chest, back, and arms were covered in these bruises, but not a mark on his hands. Not even one. It was as if whoever beat him went out of his way to avoid hitting his hands. If I were attacked with a stick or whip, I would use my hands to protect my face and there would be cuts and bruises. Don't you find that strange?"

Murphy dipped a shortbread cookie into his tea and popped it into his mouth.

"What did you charge them?" he said.

"Two dollars, but they gave me a twenty-dollar gold piece."

"Do you still have it?"

"Yes."

"Let me see it."

Hobbs dug into his vest pocket and produced the coin. He gave it to Murphy, who gave it a quick inspection. The he dug out a twenty-dollar note and set it on the table.

"I'll exchange this note for your coin," Murphy said.

"Why?" Hobbs asked.

"Because mine is real."

Murphy picked up a few extra items at the general store and then left Silver Springs to the south and easily picked up the wagon tracks followed closely by two horses. He figured that Ito, unable to ride, was in back of the wagon, Kyoto was driving, and his two bodyguards were bringing up the rear.

There was three hours of daylight left. He would ride until dusk and make camp and get an early start in the morning.

Traveling by wagon with an injured man in tow would slow them down some and Murphy was feeling optimistic about catching Kyoto before he reached Santa Fe. If Kyoto boarded a train west he could be in California in fifteen hours or so. If that happened he would be gone forever and free to launch whatever plot he was hatching.

Before he left Silver Springs, he posted his latest letter to Sally. It would take nearly a week to reach her and hopefully by then he would be able to write her with some good news.

Close to dusk, Murphy chose a spot to make camp for the night. He tied Boyle to a large brush and walked out a bit to scout the wagon tracks. Kyoto was still headed for

Santa Fe, but was moving west toward the Rio Grande.

Kyoto had some decent maps. He was traveling close to water and away from major towns and outposts. That would slow him down even more. Strange behavior for a man looking to escape the country.

Stranger still was delaying yourself even more by beating Ito and then stopping to care for the man and travel by wagon.

Murphy returned to Boyle and removed the saddle. He made a campfire and put on some beans and bacon and a pot of coffee, and then gave Boyle a good brushing while the food cooked.

"We'll get an early start tomorrow," Murphy said as he ran the brush across Boyle's back. "Right now, let's eat. I'll hobble you later."

The night sky was so clear that Murphy could see a million stars overhead as he lay in his bedroll.

The moon wouldn't rise until later and when it did its brightness would obscure many of the stars now visible, but for the moment Murphy felt as if he were looking at divinity.

Something was tugging at him and he came to realize what it was since he'd been on the trail again.

He wanted to marry Sally and have a child, maybe two. And as soon as possible because neither of them was getting any younger. When the child came of school age he didn't want the other kids thinking it was their child's grandpa walking him or her to school.

Murphy closed his eyes thinking about Sally.

About going home to her and starting life anew.

When he opened his eyes again it was with the feeling of cold, razor-sharp steel at his throat.

CHAPTER TWENTY-ONE

One of Kyoto's bodyguards, dressed in the traditional warrior garb of the samurai, held his sword to Murphy's throat.

Murphy looked up at him.

"Move and I will cut you ear-to-ear," the bodyguard said.

Murphy stayed motionless.

"Stand slowly," the bodyguard said.

With the edge of the blade against his throat, Murphy slowly stood up from the bedroll.

"Toss your weapon to the ground," the bodyguard said.

Murphy moved his right hand toward the Peacemaker.

"Two fingers on the butt," the bodyguard said.

Using two fingers, Murphy gently eased the Peacemaker from the holster and dropped it to the ground.

Murphy and the bodyguard held eye

contact for many long seconds.

"Now what?" Murphy said.

The handle of the sword was made of thick steel and the bodyguard smashed Murphy in the jaw with it and the powerful blow knocked Murphy to his knees.

"Now we see if you are the man I think you are," the bodyguard said.

He replaced the thirty-inch-long blade into the sheath on his belt, turned, and walked to his horse and tied one end of a long rope to the saddle horn. The other end he brought to Murphy and looped it around Murphy's chest.

Dazed from the heavy blow to his jaw, Murphy tried to stand, but his head spun and he sank back to his knees.

The bodyguard mounted his horse, tugged on the reins, and raced away, dragging Murphy behind him as if Murphy were a little girl's rag doll.

Boyle, still hobbled, tried to rear up on his hind legs but was unable to do so. He twisted and turned, but the leather strips around his legs held. He snorted in anger.

The bodyguard dragged Murphy across the hard ground for thirty yards, turned, and raced back to Murphy's campsite, turned again, and repeated the zigzag pattern three more times.

Satisfied that Murphy was helpless, the bodyguard stopped his horse and dismounted.

He walked to Murphy.

Murphy was on his back and appeared barely conscious.

The bodyguard walked to Boyle and tried to pat his neck, but Boyle snorted loudly and showed his teeth.

"The question is what to do with this fine horse?" the bodyguard said.

The bodyguard walked back to Murphy stood and looked down at him.

"Mr. Kyoto told me to tell you goodbye from him," the bodyguard said.

As the bodyguard grabbed the handle of his sword, Murphy came to life and brought his knees to his chest and then pumped both feet forward and smashed the bodyguard in his kneecaps with the heels of his heavy boots.

Both kneecaps shattered, the bodyguard screamed and sank to his knees and pitched forward onto his hands.

Murphy slowly stood and walked to his Peacemaker and holstered it. He returned to the incapacitated bodyguard. He looked up and tried not to show pain in his eyes and glared at Murphy.

"Never hesitate," Murphy said. "It gives

your opponent time to recuperate."

The bodyguard glared defiantly at Murphy.

"You expect me to kill you now, don't you?" Murphy said.

"Give me my honor," the bodyguard said.

Murphy stared at the bodyguard for a moment. Then he kicked him in the jaw and knocked him senseless.

"To hell with your honor," Murphy said.

From the saddle, Murphy looked at the bodyguard.

"I left you the food and water you had on your mount," Murphy said. "I'm taking him for a few miles and then I'll release him. You won't get very far crawling on your belly, so your best bet is to hope someone comes along and helps you out. And, I'll tell Kyoto goodbye myself."

Holding the reins to the bodyguard's horse, Murphy rode away. He got about a hundred yards when the bodyguard's screams gave him pause and he turned around.

Holding his sword in two hands, the bodyguard was slicing his stomach open.

A few miles south, Murphy dismounted and removed the saddle and bit from the bodyguard's horse.

He whacked the horse on the rump.

"Go on now," Murphy said.

The horse took off running and Murphy watched him for a few seconds, then mounted Boyle and continued riding.

The wagon tracks took Murphy closer to the Rio Grande River. After a few more hours' ride, he reached a long, shallow tributary of the Grande.

"We missed breakfast so this is as good a spot as any to noon," Murphy said.

He dismounted, feeling the aches and pains suffered at the hands of the bodyguard's rope.

He removed Boyle's saddle and gave him a double ration of grain. Then he built a fire and set out a pan of beans and bacon to cook, and a pot of coffee to boil.

While lunch cooked, Murphy removed all his clothing, grabbed a bar of soap from the saddlebags, and found a shallow spot on the riverbank and dove in headfirst.

After a few minutes of scrubbing, Murphy emerged clean and a bit less sore from the cold water. He dressed in front of the fire and sat down to eat.

The hot food stung his chafed, swollen lips.

He ate quickly and then added several ounces of his father's whiskey to a cup of coffee. The hot, whiskey-laced coffee burned his throat, but after a few seconds worked its magic and eased some of the sting.

Murphy stood and sipped from the cup as he rubbed Boyle's neck.

"Our choices are to push on until dark, or stay here and rest," he said. "If we rest, Kyoto gets that much closer to Santa Fe. He's headed west toward the Rio Grande and could make Santa Fe in two days, so what do you think?"

Boyle snorted and turned his head to look at Murphy.

Murphy gave him a few sugar cubes.

"You're right," Murphy said. "Plenty of time to rest when the job is done."

Murphy returned to the fire for more coffee and whiskey. He dug out his maps and studied them for a few minutes.

Raton was less than six hours ride to the southwest. He could make it by sundown, sleep in a bed, and get an early start in the morning.

He looked at Boyle.

"I know what you're thinking," Murphy said. "By now Kyoto realizes his man isn't coming back and might send out the other one. I don't think he'll do that and risk being unprotected with an injured man. Besides, they have a telegraph in Raton and I really could use a hot bath and a warm bed."

A few miles from the town of Raton in northern New Mexico, Murphy rode across the site for the new rail line being constructed by the Santa Fe and Topeka railroads. It was to be a short line for mining operations. From a distance, Murphy estimated the line was still six months or more from completion.

A hundred men or so were working on the rails. In the background, the Raton Mountain Range extended as far as the eye could see.

The day's work was done and the men were headed toward the chow tent when Murphy rode into the encampment.

Several men armed with Winchester rifles and Colt pistols quickly approached Murphy as he dismounted.

"This is a private railroad camp," one of the men said.

"I know that," Murphy said. "Who is your chief of police?"

From behind Murphy, a man said, "That would be me."

Murphy turned and looked at Swan, Chief

of Railroad Police on the Santa Fe to Dodge City line when it was under construction.

"Thought I recognized you from a mile off," Swan said as he extended his right hand to Murphy.

"Good to see you again," Murphy said as they shook.

"Men, this here is Mr. Murphy," Swan said. "You've all heard the stories. Here he is in the flesh."

"Got a place where we can talk?" Murphy said.

"My tent," Swan said.

"Who is railroad boss on this project?" Murphy asked.

Bradley poked his head into Swan's tent and smiled at Murphy.

"It is you," Bradley said as he came in and offered his right hand to Murphy.

They shook and Murphy said, "I have about three shots left in the bottle of my father's whiskey, care to join us?"

"Don't mind if I do, and if I may, Parker is making fried chicken for dinner tonight," Bradley said. "Mr. Swan, the offer includes you as well."

"Don't mind if I do," Swan said.

Murphy filled the three shot glasses on the table beside Swan's bunk and handed one to Bradley and Swan.

"To fried chicken," Murphy said and tossed back his shot.

Parker, once a slave to a wealthy, Georgia plantation owner, was trained in the finer arts of cooking, and served and worked for Bradley for a dozen years or more. When they weren't on the road building new lines, Parker lived with Bradley's family and served as the family chef. After setting plates for four and bringing chicken, potatoes, carrots, breads, and iced tea to the table, Parker took his seat at Bradley's right hand.

"It's nice to see you again, Mr. Murphy," Parker said.

"It's nice to eat your cooking again, Mr. Parker," Murphy said.

"So what brings you west again?" Bradley asked Murphy.

Murphy dug out his wallet and removed a counterfeit twenty-dollar bill and set it before Bradley.

"It's a long story, but an interesting one," Murphy said.

By the time the table was cleared and Parker served coffee and dessert, Murphy had wrapped up his tale.

Swan held the counterfeit bill.

"I can't believe this is fake money," he said.

"The favor I have to ask is a large one," Murphy said to Bradley.

"Ask," Bradley said.

"I need you to ride with me to Raton and send a telegram to the home office in Santa Fe," Murphy said. "I need the Santa Fe to shut down its line from Santa Fe west and south for at least a week."

"A week?" Bradley said. "They've just repaired the burned-out track. Schedules are off a week or more as it is."

"If Kyoto is allowed to reach California, he will disappear on the first schooner back to Japan," Murphy said.

Bradley sighed. "All right," he said. "Mr. Swan, could you have my horse saddled and please accompany us to Raton?"

"You got me out of bed, now what is it you want to say?" the telegraph operator snarled at Bradley.

Bradley handed the operator the note he prepared earlier.

The operator read it and then looked at Bradley.

"Is this for real, Mr. Bradley?" he said.

"Afraid so," Bradley said.

"All right," the operator said. "Will you

wait for a reply?"

"I'll be across the street in the saloon," Bradley said. "Bring it to me there."

Murphy, Bradley, and Swan were drinking coffee at a table in the saloon when the telegraph operator came in with Bradley's reply.

"Please have a seat," Bradley said. "Help yourself to a cup."

While Bradley read the reply, the operator filled a mug from the pot on the table and took a chair.

"I'll have you know that was the longest telegram I have ever sent," the operator said. "More words than the Gettysburg Address."

"Couldn't be helped," Bradley said as he passed the reply to Murphy.

Murphy scanned it quickly and set the paper on the table.

"I need to alert the president," he said.

"Alert the . . . who are you, anyway?" the operator said.

"This is Mr. Murphy," Bradley said. "He is a federal agent."

"I need to borrow your telegraph station," Murphy said.

"What do you mean borrow?" the operator asked.

"My wire is classified," Murphy said. "I'll

send it myself."

"Western Union rules state . . ." the operator said.

"No use arguing with him," Bradley said.

Murphy stood up from the table. "I won't be long," he said. "Order another pot of coffee."

To William Burke The White House Stop From Murphy Stop I have shut down the Santa Fe Railroad west to prevent suspected counterfeiter Ren Norio Kyoto from traveling to California and leaving the country Stop Have Customs and immigration revoke Kyoto's diplomatic status immediately Stop No reply Stop Murphy

Murphy was about to stand up from the operator's table when he decided to send a second telegram.

To William Burke The White House Stop What is the status of Sally's relocation to Tennessee home Stop Please reply Stop Murphy.

"Is there a hotel or boarding house in town where I can spend the night?" Murphy asked the operator.

"Hotel?" the operator said. "Where do you think you are, Santa Fe? We don't even have a full-time sheriff here."

"You can stay in my spare room in my train," Bradley said.

"I'll be awhile," Murphy said. "I need to wait for a reply."

"Lock the door when you're done," the operator said. "I'm going back to bed."

To Murphy Stop From W Burke Stop Sally has left Washington Stop All is well Stop She will contact me soon Stop Burke

Even though Murphy wrote the response himself, he read the message twice, then folded it and tucked it into his shirt pocket.

He returned to the saloon where Bradley and Swan were still at the table.

"Mr. Bradley, I'll take you up on that invitation now," Murphy said.

CHAPTER TWENTY-TWO

Murphy and Bradley studied Bradley's highly detailed maps in the office car of Bradley's private railroad cars.

Each man had a snifter of brandy.

"His other option would be to continue west and south to Flagstaff, but he would have to cross eighty miles of desert and this time of year that's nearly suicide," Bradley said.

"Kyoto is not crazy," Murphy said. "Once he finds out the railroad has shut down service, he'll either continue south to find another route, or . . . head east and north," Murphy said.

"To where?"

Murphy scanned the maps.

"He could get the railroad in Dodge City and Amarillo, Texas," Murphy said. "Or . . . continue south to Mexico."

Murphy paused to flip pages in Bradley's maps.

"The railroad in Juárez just over the border is an American investment, isn't it?" Murphy asked.

Bradley nodded. "With clear track all the way to Baja and north to San Diego."

Murphy stared at the maps.

"And a ticket to a schooner back to Japan," Murphy said.

"Maybe he doesn't know that?" Bradley said. "He could be lost in the desert for all we know."

Murphy took a small sip of his brandy. "He is too smart for that," he said. "I don't think there isn't one thing that he doesn't plan before executing."

"Except that even the best of plans can go astray by circumstances," Bradley said. "Such as Apaches burning railroad tracks."

Murphy nodded as he looked at the maps.

"He'll go south to Santa Fe before making his decision on what to do next," Murphy said. "If . . . if he believes the Santa Fe line will open up in a few days he might stick around to catch it."

Bradley sipped his brandy and looked at the maps.

"What are you going to do?" he asked.

"Ask me that in the morning after I've had some sleep," Murphy said.

Bradley looked at the clock on the wall.

"Yes, it's after midnight," he said. "I'm sure you're exhausted. We both could use a good night's sleep. Parker will have a full breakfast waiting in the morning."

Burke tossed and turned in his bed until finally he gave up and decided to have a brandy to help him sleep.

Wearing slippers and a robe, he went downstairs to his study and lit the oil lantern mounted on the wall, then filled a snifter with brandy and sat on the leather chair beside his library.

He lied to Murphy about Sally's status and that weighed heavily upon his mind.

To be sure, losing Sally would be a heavy blow for Murphy to absorb, but the country always has and always will come first and foremost in Burke's mind.

Murphy would agree with that if Sally had never entered his life and he had an unbiased opinion.

But, she did, and he might not see it the same as Burke anymore.

Love changed a man.

Gave him new perspectives he never knew existed. Wife and family became priority one and duty to country took the back seat on the buggy.

Knowing Murphy's history, how he lost

his wife and son during the war, the decade plus of guilt and loneliness, the loss of Sally would not bode well once he learned the news.

And even then, Burke wasn't sure if he could tell Murphy all of it.

Burke sipped brandy and wondered what to do.

Union Station in Chicago was the most massive building Sally had ever seen and that included the train station in Saint Louis and Philadelphia.

It wasn't just large, but almost cathedral-like in appearance.

Tiled floors, stained-glass windows, polished brass clock centered in the terminal waiting area, even shops and restaurants, although none were open at this hour.

Almost midnight, passengers waiting for trains were few. Sally counted seven people in the waiting area. They had to be waiting for the midnight train to Minnesota, which made dozens of stops in Wisconsin along the way.

Her final destination was Ontario, Canada. One of her girls from the Saint Louis brothel was from Canada, and a year ago she married a wealthy businessman from Ontario who frequented Saint Louis on business and she relocated with him.

Sally had no need for their money. She had twenty-thousand dollars in bank drafts that she could deposit into any Canadian bank. What she needed was guidance in relocating and finding a residence where she could have her baby and raise it properly.

If her child was to grow up without a father it would be of her choosing and not because he rotted in prison or died at the hands of a hangman.

She loved Murphy with all her heart and soul, but she had to leave him to save his life, or worse, a miserable existence in prison. If he were a more reasonable man, maybe he might seek to have Christopher arrested for what he did, but having witnessed Murphy's power and demeanor on the trail, she knew that he would simply kill Christopher and be done with it.

"Miss, are you all right?"

Sally looked up at the Chicago policeman standing before her. He wore a blue uniform and carried a stick on the end of a leather strip.

She was about to answer and then she realized that she was crying.

"Miss?" the policeman said.

"I'm fine," Sally said. "I recently lost my . . . husband. I was . . . missing him. I'm fine. Thank you for asking."

"Are you waiting on the twelve-fifteen train?" the policeman asked.

"Yes."

"I'll wait with you until it arrives," the policeman said. "Where are your bags?"

"I checked them with a porter," Sally said. "He'll take them on for me."

"Just the same, I'll stay with you until they call for boarding," the policeman said.

Sally nodded. "Thank you."

Burke had another brandy and lit one of his Cuban cigars to accompany it. He sat in his leather chair and thought about Kyoto.

As Murphy requested, Kyoto's diplomatic status was revoked. That wouldn't prevent Kyoto's passage out of the country if he reached a schooner on the west coast, but it did make it easier to detain him if captured.

Counterfeiting was a federal crime. Perpetrated by a foreign dignitary was a far worse offense. If the diplomat was acting with the authority of his government, it could even be interpreted as an act of war.

And that wasn't acceptable.

There was no room for error on this.

Burke sipped brandy and puffed on the cigar.

He made the decision to hide Sally's leaving until after Murphy's work was done. It was the only way to ensure Murphy's dedication to the job didn't waver.

He would deal with the truth when Murphy returned from the field.

And accept the consequences.

If Grant were still in the White House, Grant would probably say the son of a bitch had it coming, and dismiss it.

Maybe even Garfield.

Chester Arthur was a complication.

As valuable a commodity as Murphy was, Arthur would not tolerate murder in his administration.

Burke sat and thought about what to do.

CHAPTER TWENTY-THREE

Parker served thick-sliced bacon and buttermilk pancakes that Murphy estimated as three-quarters of an inch thick. Fresh baked biscuits, coffee, and juice were also on the table.

"Mr. Parker, if you ever get tired of railroad life, you can come work for me in Tennessee," Murphy said. "Me and the missus."

Bradley cocked an eyebrow at Murphy. "That would be Sally Orr?"

"It would," Murphy said. "As soon as I'm done with this assignment, we're to be married."

"I'm delighted to hear the news," Bradley said.

"May we attend the ceremony?" Parker asked. "I would consider it an honor to prepare the food and bake a wedding cake."

"Tennessee is a long way off," Murphy said.

"What's the fun of having your own private train if you can't use it once in a while?" Bradley said.

"I'll wire you the invite," Murphy said.

"Excellent," Bradley said.

"Mr. Bradley, Mr. Murphy, you better get out here quick!" Swan called from outside the train.

Murphy stood and pulled his Peacemaker and walked to the door. He pointed to Parker. "Stay put," he said.

Murphy opened the door and stepped out to the platform of the railroad car and looked down at Swan.

Swan held a Winchester rifle and used it to point to a hill about three-hundred yards away.

"Are we under attack?" Swan asked.

Murphy looked at Ten Moons and his son, Two Bears. They were in Apache garb atop their massive horses, motionless the way only an Apache can sit.

"Only if we're out of sugar," Murphy said.

"What?" Swan said.

Murphy poked his head into the car.

"Mr. Parker, two more for breakfast," he said.

"I like these pancakes," Ten Moons said.

"More?" Parker asked.

"Yes."

"Father, you have to watch your weight," Two Bears said. "You're not getting any younger, you know."

"Forgive my son," Ten Moons said. "He went to your medical school and now he thinks he knows everything."

"You went to medical school?" Bradley asked.

"Back east," Two Bears said.

"You're that Apache doctor who works at the Army fort?" Bradley said. "I've heard of you."

Two Bears nodded as he sliced into a stack of pancakes.

"Would you like some coffee?" Parker asked.

"Do you have sugar?" Ten Moons said.

"Of course."

"I will have your coffee," Ten Moons said.

Murphy stuffed his pipe as he looked at Ten Moons. "Not that I'm not delighted to see my old friend again so soon, but what are you doing here?"

"Your word has great power," Ten Moons said. "My son was released from prison and the Army and your government has apologized and also added funds for his hospital."

"And you rode all this way to tell me that?" Murphy asked.

"We, my son and I, are here to join your hunt for the foreigners," Ten Moons said. "To show my respect for your word."

Two Bears looked at Murphy. "No use trying to talk him out of it," he said.

"Only an Apache can track in this country," Ten Moons said.

Parker set a coffee cup in front of Ten Moons.

"Sugar is already in it," Parker said.

"I'll go saddle my horse," Murphy said.

"Can it wait until I finish my pancakes?" Ten Moons asked.

Murphy struck a match and lit his pipe. "Why not?"

"Say, doctor, maybe you can have a look at my bunion?" Parker asked Two Bears. "My feet are killing me."

"South and west to Santa Fe," Ten Moons said, as he inspected wagon tracks in the dry dirt. "One rider behind the wagon."

"How far ahead do you figure?" Murphy asked atop Boyle.

"Three days at most."

"They will reach Santa Fe sometime tonight," Murphy said.

"And catch the railroad?" Ten Moons said.

"No," Murphy said. "I had the railroad shut down."

Ten Moons looked at Murphy as he stood up.

"Your word is greater than your chiefs in Washington," he said.

"They're not my chiefs," Murphy said. "My chief was Grant and he's retired. Let's go. We need to make time."

Close to dark, Ten Moons dismounted at a campsite. He knelt and stirred the ashes of a fire.

"Two days," he said.

"Make camp," Murphy said. "We'll get an early start in the morning."

"It's not the Apache way to abandon a hunt when there is still daylight."

"It's not the Apache way to eat pancakes for breakfast, either," Murphy said.

"I'll get some firewood," Two Bears said.

Eating plates of beans, bacon, and biscuits around the campfire, Murphy spread out his maps and reviewed them with Ten Moons and Two Bears.

"With no railroad, they will turn west at Santa Fe," Murphy said. "That's my guess."

"Why?" Two Bears asked.

"They can't risk heading south to Mexico through six-hundred miles of desert country to cross the border to catch the railroad

275

west," Murphy said. "Especially knowing they're being pursued. Once Kyoto finds out the railroad is shut down, he'll head into Arizona where it's less likely he'll run into the law on the way to Flagstaff where he can catch a train west."

"Hard country, Arizona," Ten Moons said.

"No worse than here, and it's a hundred miles closer," Murphy said. "He'll resupply in Santa Fe and head to Flagstaff. I'm sure of it."

"We should make Santa Fe in forty hours," Two Bears said. "It will be difficult to pick up their trail west from there if they cross the Grande into desert country, especially if they have a two-day head start."

"I thought about sending a wire to the sheriff's office in Santa Fe, but the sheriff and his deputy are new to the job," Murphy said. "Kyoto's man is a highly skilled killer. What they call a samurai warrior in Japan. Much like an Apache warrior in America."

"There were four," Ten Moons said.

"I wounded one of them a few days ago and he took his own life rather than face the shame of defeat," Murphy said.

Ten Moons and Two Bears looked at each other.

"You mean suicide?" Two Bears said.

"Not in the traditional sense," Murphy

said. "Honor and disgrace mean everything to the Japanese people. If the shame is too great to regain your honor, it's expected that you sacrifice your life."

"They don't fear death," Ten Moons said.

"No."

"That makes them a dangerous enemy," Ten Moons said. "Like the Apache."

"Yes," Murphy said. "Like the Apache."

"And you think this warrior would kill the sheriff in Santa Fe?" Two Bears said.

"If he had to, yes," Murphy said. "I'm hoping Kyoto rides into town quietly, finds out the railroad is down, picks up supplies, and rides out just as quietly."

"The station is on the edge of town," Two Bears said.

"Away from the center, yes," Murphy said. "So one man can sneak in for supplies and then slip out quietly."

"I look forward to meeting this warrior," Ten Moons said.

"Father, this isn't Little Big Horn," Two Bears said. "And besides, I think Mr. Murphy would prefer taking his prisoners alive."

"You think?" Ten Moons said. "What I think is that you should hold your tongue and pour me more coffee."

Six hours from Santa Fe, Murphy spotted

something a mile or more away on the horizon. He paused and dug out the binoculars and zoomed in on the dot and it was a wagon.

"Looks like they abandoned the wagon to make better time," Murphy said.

"Let me see your spyglass," Ten Moons said.

Murphy passed him the binoculars.

"Less conspicuous to leave your horse outside of town and walk to the railroad station," Murphy said.

"I must get a spyglass," Ten Moons said. "For hunting game."

"That's not the Apache way, Father," Two Bears said.

Ten Moons gave the binoculars back to Murphy and then turned to look at Two Bears. "Neither is spanking a full-grown son," he said.

Murphy dismounted and approached the wagon. It was loaded with supplies.

"They left their goods," he said. "Because at this point they don't know the railroad is down."

"They couldn't be more than eighteen hours ahead of us when they left the wagon," Two Bears said.

Murphy riffled through the supplies.

"There's plenty we can use right here," he said. "We'll only need a few things in town."

Ten Moons and Two Bears dismounted and between the three of them loading goods into their saddlebags they emptied the wagon.

"What is this box?" Ten Moons said as he held up a small box.

"Japanese tea," Murphy said.

Ten Moons opened the small, wood box and felt the tea leaves. "Can you smoke it in your pipe?"

"You can, but I don't advise it," Murphy said. "Let's go."

The ticket office at the Santa Fe railroad station was crowded with angry people demanding to know why the trains were shut down.

A distraught railroad employee did his best to explain things to the mob of people demanding answers.

"All I can tell you is service on the Santa Fe line west and south has been suspended until further notice," he said. "Hanging around here, yelling at me, won't fix the problem. I'll post a notice the minute service is restored."

Slowly the crowd left the office until Murphy was left standing alone.

The railroad employee looked at Murphy. "I'll tell you what I told the others," he said. "The . . ."

"I heard," Murphy said and flashed his identification. "I'm looking for a wanted man who might have tried to buy a ticket in the last day or so."

"You saw the crowd," the employee said. "I must have seen two-hundred faces in the last two days. I can't remember one from the other."

"You'd remember him," Murphy said. "He's Japanese. Tall. Long dark hair. Powerfully built."

The employee stared at Murphy for a moment. "Yesterday morning, I saw a man outside the office that fits that description," he said.

"Did he come inside?"

"No. No need, I suppose. Signs posted and there were enough angry people out there for him to hear the train was shut down."

"Thank you," Murphy said.

Holding Boyle by the reins, Murphy walked into town and tied Boyle to the post outside the sheriff's office.

A young man wearing a deputy's badge was behind the desk.

He stood up when Murphy entered.

"I'm Deputy Spooner, can I help you?"

Murphy pointed to the coffee pot on the Franklin stove. "Is there hot coffee in that pot?"

"There is."

Murphy flashed his identification and then filled a tin cup with hot coffee and then took the chair opposite the desk.

"Who is sheriff now in Santa Fe?" he said.

"That would be Sheriff Gwynn," Spooner said.

"I think it's best if you found Sheriff Gwynn so I don't have to tell my story twice," Murphy said and sipped from the cup. "You make good coffee, by the way."

Murphy sipped coffee and said, "Kyoto came into town probably early. I tracked him here. He came in yesterday morning. Did you or the deputy see him?"

"No, but we were gone most of the day," Gwynn said. "We had business out of town with some ranchers and rustlers stealing cattle. We left before dawn and didn't return until after dark."

Murphy nodded.

"He needs supplies," he said. "How many general stores in town?"

Kyoto's bodyguard purchased supplies for

two weeks at the general store closest to the railroad station.

The clerk behind the counter said, "Of course I remember him. How many Japanese men do you think I get in my store in a given year?"

"I'll need some supplies myself," Murphy said. "Let me have three gallon canteens, ten pounds of beans, a bag of salt, flour, ten pounds of jerky, five pounds of coffee, ten pounds of salt bacon, a pouch of tobacco, sugar, and a dozen bars of that Swiss chocolate you have there under the counter. Pack it in a couple of sacks I can hang off my saddle."

Leaving the store with his goods, Murphy said to Gwynn, "Where is your public well? I'd like to fill up these canteens."

Murphy joined Ten Moons and Two Bears a half-mile west of Santa Fe.

"We picked up their tracks," Two Bears said. "They're headed west as you said."

"You're sure?" Murphy said.

"One of them sits his horse too far forward in the saddle," Ten Moons said. "His horse is uncomfortable."

"That would be Kyoto," Murphy said. "How far ahead of us?"

"Day and a half," Two Bears said.

"They don't know the country," Ten Moons said. "We can catch up to them in four to five days."

Murphy nodded. "Let's go," he said.

CHAPTER TWENTY-FOUR

"This is hard country," Ten Moons said.

"We're in Arizona," Murphy said. "A few hours and we'll reach what we call the Petrified Forest."

"I studied about it in school," Two Bears said. "I've never seen."

"I have," Ten Moons said. "It is not easy country to cross."

"If you're in a hurry to get to Flagstaff, the quickest way is through the Petrified Forest," Murphy said. "It will be dark by the time we reach the entrance. We'll make camp and ride through in daylight."

"Tell me why this fake money is so important to the chiefs in Washington," Ten Moons said.

"A lot of reasons," Murphy said. "The entire economic system of America is based upon its currency."

"I don't understand the word economic,"

Ten Moons said.

Murphy stirred the beans and bacon in the fry pan. "Say that you had thirty ponies and that made you a rich man because ponies were hard to come by. If somebody let loose thousands of wild ponies and they were everywhere, and everybody had them, your thirty wouldn't be worth much anymore because they were now common. Understand?"

Ten Moons nodded. "I think I do."

When the food was ready, Murphy filled three plates and they continued talking as they ate.

"So whatever plot Kyoto is up to concerning counterfeit money is of vital interest to Washington and the country," Murphy said.

"So we need to capture him alive to find out this information?" Ten Moons said.

"Exactly," Murphy said.

"The coffee is ready if you want some, Father," Two Bears said.

Murphy filled three cups and added some sugar to sweeten Ten Moons's cup.

"I have something for you," Murphy said.

Murphy dug out three chocolate bars from his saddlebags and gave one to Ten Moons and Two Bears.

"Dark chocolate from Switzerland," Murphy said.

Murphy opened the wrapper on his bar and took a bite.

Ten Moons looked at the chocolate bar in his hand, peeled back the wrapper, and snapped a piece off.

"Eat it, Father," Two Bears said. "It's good. I've had some at the fort."

Ten Moons put the piece into his mouth and chewed. His eyes widened and he nodded to Murphy.

"What is Switz . . . land?" he said.

"Switzerland, and it's a country in Europe across the ocean," Murphy said. "Try this."

Murphy snapped off a piece of chocolate and put it into his coffee. He swirled the chocolate around with his finger to melt it and then took a sip.

Ten Moons did the same and then he sipped from his cup.

"I had rock candy once at a trading post near an Army fort," he said. "This is much better."

"I agree," Murphy said. "Much better."

Murphy and Ten Moons inspected the tracks a few hundred yards into the Petrified Forest.

"What is he up to?" Murphy asked.

Two Bears dismounted and knelt beside Murphy.

"What?" Two Bears said.

"They split up," Murphy said. "Two horses went straight into the desert canyons, the third veered off to the right to those hills."

"We need to split up," Two Bears said.

"We will track the two," Ten Moons said.

"All right, but you watch yourself," Murphy said. "Kyoto is nobody's fool. We'll meet in two days at the end of the forest."

Murphy figured he was following the tracks made by Kyoto's second bodyguard. Kyoto must have thought splitting up would make it more difficult for Murphy to follow, not realizing Murphy was no longer tracking alone.

He figured to walk into a trap set by the bodyguard and the easiest way to get taken by surprise was on horseback. Higher off the ground, unable to see tracks and signs as clearly, and open to attack from above, Murphy dismounted and led Boyle up a gentle hill to higher ground.

The trap would have to be soon to be effective. Kyoto still had a day's ride head start, so the bodyguard would have to be near enough to spring the trap and still be able to catch up to Kyoto inside of a day.

Murphy knelt before a set of tracks that

led to higher ground. He tied Boyle to some brush and took the Winchester rifle out of the saddle sleeve.

"I won't be long," Murphy said and patted Boyle's neck.

He ascended the hill about two-hundred feet where it leveled off to flat ground. The tracks continued in a straight line across the rugged terrain and after a hundred yards or so, Murphy came across a large pile of dung.

He knelt, picked up a twig, and poked the dung. The core was soft, not more than a few hours old.

Murphy stood and looked backwards.

"Ten Moons," he said aloud.

Ten Moons and Two Bears followed the two sets of tracks through the rocky, mountainous terrain into a narrow gorge.

They dismounted and inspected tracks.

"The one who leans forward is riding first," Ten Moons said.

"Up ahead they dismounted and started walking," Two Bears said.

Ten Moons looked up to the top of the gorge.

"I'm going for a look," he said. "Stay with the horses."

"Be quick about it," Two Bears said. "I don't like it here."

"You take after your mother," Ten Moons said, and started to climb the cliff to their right.

Two Bears watched as Ten Moons ascended several hundred yards to the top and vanished as he reached the summit.

"Yeah, well, mother would never be so stupid," Two Bears said.

About ten minutes passed and Two Bears removed the canteen from his horse to take a drink. As he held the canteen high and sipped, the horses nervously whinnied and he turned around and looked at the imposing figure of the bodyguard.

Dressed in some sort of ritual garb, the bodyguard held a long curved sword.

Two Bears lowered the canteen. He made and held eye contact with the bodyguard for several long seconds.

Twenty feet separated them.

The bodyguard slowly brought the sword overhead.

Two Bears dropped the canteen.

The bodyguard rushed forward.

Two Bears pulled the Winchester from the saddle sleeve and cocked the lever.

Before Two Bears could aim, the bodyguard was upon him and slashed downward with the sword.

Two Bears used the Winchester to block

the sword and it fired a bullet into the ground at his feet.

The bodyguard slashed out with the sword and knocked the Winchester from Two Bears's hands, and Two Bears grabbed the tomahawk on his belt.

The bodyguard slashed out with the sword again and Two Bears was able to use the tomahawk to block the razor-sharp blade, but a tomahawk was no match for thirty inches of steel and soon the bodyguard had Two Bears on the defensive and backing up.

Two Bears attacked with the tomahawk and the bodyguard sidestepped it and sliced the sword across Two Bears's naked stomach.

As blood gushed from the deep cut, Two Bears froze and the bodyguard sliced down at Two Bears's right wrist and cut off the hand at the bone.

Two Bears looked at his right hand on the ground, which still clutched the tomahawk.

The bodyguard spun around and swung the sword and cut Two Bears at the neck and Two Bears slunk to his knees and fell to his face.

At the sound of the Winchester rifle firing, Ten Moons turned and raced back down the gorge wall. He pulled his tomahawk at the sight of Two Bears on the ground with the bodyguard standing over him.

Ten Moons screamed as he slid the last twenty feet to the ground.

The bodyguard was ready for Ten Moons's charge.

Ten Moons attacked with the tomahawk, but he had never seen a samurai sword and had no idea how to defend against the powerful weapon.

The bodyguard spun and opened a cut on Ten Moons's stomach with the tip of the sword.

Ten Moons slashed out with the tomahawk and the bodyguard blocked it with the sword, spun again, and cut a long gash into Ten Moons's left thigh.

Ten Moons ignored the pain and blood and charged the bodyguard with the tomahawk and the bodyguard blocked the tomahawk, spun, and cut Ten Moons across the chest.

The cut was deep and the tomahawk fell from Ten Moons's hand.

Ten Moons looked down at the lifeless body of his son.

The eyes of the bodyguard locked onto Ten Moons and never wavered.

Ten Moons pulled his knife, held it high

above his head, screamed the Apache war cry, and charged the bodyguard.

The bodyguard let Ten Moons get within striking distance and then shoved the sword into his stomach and held fast.

Ten Moons looked at the sword and then stared defiantly at the bodyguard.

The bodyguard's eyes locked onto Ten Moons's icy stare as he sliced open his stomach and then withdrew the sword.

As Ten Moons collapsed to the ground, the bodyguard wiped the blood from his sword on the back of Ten Moons's horse, and then replaced it into the sheath on his belt.

As the bodyguard walked away, Ten Moons crawled on his belly to Two Bears and with his dying breath, reached out to touch his son's face.

As Murphy raced back to Boyle, a crack of a rifle sounded and for a split second he froze in place.

"No," Murphy said and ran down the hill to Boyle, and in one swift motion leapt onto Boyle's rear and into the saddle.

"Go!" Murphy shouted and took the reins in his left hand as he held the Winchester in his right.

He ran Boyle as fast as the horse could go

and backtracked into the canyon and yanked
Boyle to a stop thirty feet from the bodies
of Ten Moons and Two Bears.

Murphy stuck the Winchester into the
saddle sleeve and slid down to the ground.

He walked to his fallen comrades and
knelt down.

"You're home now," Murphy said and
touched Ten Moons on the cheek. "Watch
over your son."

Murphy stood and returned to Boyle and
opened one of the saddlebags and removed
a fifteen-foot-long leather whip and draped
it over the saddle horn.

Then he took the reins and looked Boyle
in the eye.

"I need you to run like you've never run
before," he said. "Like it was your last day
on Earth."

He put his foot into the stirrup and as if
he understood Murphy's commands, the
moment Murphy was in the saddle, Boyle
snorted loudly and ran.

CHAPTER TWENTY-FIVE

Murphy ran Boyle along the ground inside the gorge for several miles until they reached the other side and when he spotted a dot on the horizon, he asked Boyle to run even harder.

"He's headed west," Murphy said, aloud. "We have to cut him off."

Murphy turned Boyle hard to the west to cut down the distance and Boyle responded by gulping in large amounts of air and snorting through his nose and forcing his powerful legs to run faster.

Slowly the gap closed to half a mile.

Boyle's chest and legs started to foam with salt.

"A few more minutes," Murphy said.

Foamy salt flew off Boyle's coat as the gap closed to five-hundred yards.

"Hold up," Murphy said and brought Boyle to a slow walk before stopping him.

He grabbed the Winchester, dismounted,

cocked the lever, and used the saddle to steady the rifle.

Murphy took careful aim, held his breath, and slowly squeezed the trigger.

Two seconds later, struck by the powerful round, the bodyguard's horse fell to the ground and the bodyguard went flying.

"God forgive me for shooting one of your creatures," Murphy said, then tucked the Winchester into the saddle sleeve and mounted Boyle.

"He's on foot now," Murphy said. "No need to run."

Murphy walked Boyle to the bodyguard. As the gap closed the one-hundred yards, the bodyguard, who had been sitting, stood and drew his sword.

Murphy stopped Boyle when the gap was twenty feet and slid out of the saddle holding the whip. Extended, the whip revealed a metal barb on the end.

The bodyguard and Murphy glared at each other.

"You no good son of a bitch," Murphy said. "Tonight you will shake hands with whatever god you believe in."

The bodyguard held the sword and stared at Murphy's Peacemaker.

"What? This?" Murphy said and drew the Peacemaker and tossed it to the ground.

As the gun made contact with the ground, the bodyguard screamed in Japanese and charged Murphy.

Murphy flicked his wrist and the metal tip of the whip lashed out and struck the bodyguard on the right cheek.

The bodyguard paused as blood appeared and ran down his face.

"That was a taste. Want more?" Murphy asked.

The bodyguard looked at the whip.

"Come on, then," Murphy said.

The bodyguard, sword at arm's length, moved forward.

Murphy snapped the whip and a deep cut appeared in the bodyguard's robe across the chest. It took a moment and then blood appeared.

The bodyguard looked at the blood.

"You killed my friend and his son," Murphy said and snapped the whip again and a second cut appeared on the bodyguard's cheek.

The bodyguard spun and charged with the sword and Murphy snapped the whip and another cut appeared on the bodyguard's chest.

"And I will have no mercy for that," Murphy said.

Murphy snapped the whip again and again

and each time the whip struck, a new cut appeared on the bodyguard's face and chest.

Bleeding from a dozen cuts, or more, the bodyguard stepped back to regroup.

Murphy knew the samurai were trained to ignore pain and injury, but he was bleeding heavily from two deep cuts to his chest and the loss of blood weakened him. He would die rather than surrender and it would come down to that for sure.

The bodyguard slowly brought the heavy sword over his head.

Twenty feet separated them.

Murphy watched his eyes.

The bodyguard charged forward, hoping to break through the defense of the whip and land a fatal blow with the sword.

As the bodyguard roared loudly and charged, Murphy went down to one knee and flicked the whip low to the ground and encircled it around the bodyguard's right ankle. Murphy stood and yanked the whip and the bodyguard fell to his back, and the sword bounced away from his grasp.

Murphy walked to the sword and picked it up and stood over the dazed bodyguard.

"Ten Moons and his son were good men," Murphy said, and held the sword to the bodyguard's throat. "This is a white man's country, but they are the backbone."

The bodyguard glared defiantly at Murphy.

Murphy turned and walked to his Peacemaker, picked it up, and holstered it. Then he tossed the sword on the ground beside the bodyguard.

"Pick it up," Murphy said.

The bodyguard slowly picked up the sword and got to his feet.

"This isn't Japan," Murphy said.

The bodyguard held the sword above his head and rushed forward.

Murphy drew the Peacemaker and shot the bodyguard three times in the chest and he fell backward dead to the ground.

"And there are no samurai in America," Murphy said and gently replaced the Peacemaker into the holster.

Murphy picked out a spot atop a flat gorge that faced the sunset and removed the folding shovel from his gear.

He dug two graves side-by-side and worked until midnight without taking a break. Then he carried Ten Moons and Two Bears up to the gorge and gently laid them to rest.

"I will tell your people how bravely you died," Murphy said. "And I give my word that the hospital will be built."

And by moonlight, Murphy covered the graves.

CHAPTER TWENTY-SIX

Sally stood in awe at the majestic sight of Lake Superior, the largest and deepest of the five Great Lakes.

Standing behind a fence, she stared out at the massive body of water and watched sailboats shimmer on the waves. She was at her last stop before entering Canada, the town of Duluth in Minnesota.

Tomorrow morning after breakfast, she would catch the railroad into Canada and meet her friend and leave America and all that she knew behind.

She turned and took a seat on a bench facing a walking path. A man of about Murphy's height, although older, was strolling arm-in-arm with his wife. They appeared very much in love and happy, and why not? They had a long, shared life together and it showed on their faces.

Her heart ached for Murphy.

Maybe it wasn't too late to turn around

and go to Tennessee? She could tell him the child was his and he would have no reason to doubt her word. Until the baby was born and he took one look at it and knew that it wasn't his.

Maybe she could convince him to forgive and forget?

She remembered the first time she saw Murphy when he rode into the Dodge railroad camp. He dismounted his giant horse and the hard-as-nails railroad men got out of his way as if he were a coiled rattlesnake ready to strike.

No, Murphy would never forgive and he would never forget.

She wiped a tear from her eye, stood, and took a final look at the lake before returning to her sleeper car on the train.

At dawn, Murphy said a Christian prayer over the graves of Ten Moons and Two Bears. He didn't know any Apache prayers, but he did speak some Apache and did his best to repeat the prayer in their native tongue.

Then he walked the horses belonging to Ten Moons and Two Bears to a clearing and set them free.

Confused, the horses looked at Murphy.

"Go on, you're free," Murphy said and

slapped one of them on the rump.

The horse took off, quickly followed by the other, and Murphy watched them run until they were nearly out of sight.

About to mount Boyle, Murphy paused for a moment, then opened a saddlebag and dug out the bag of sugar. He stood over the grave of Ten Moons and sprinkled some sugar onto the dirt.

Then he packed the sugar away, mounted Boyle, and rode west off the gorge.

Around one in the afternoon, Murphy noticed a slight limp in Boyle's front left leg. He stopped and made camp for lunch.

"My fault for running you so hard," Murphy said.

He dug out a bottle of liniment from a saddlebag and rubbed the leg thoroughly.

"Let that set awhile," Murphy said.

Murphy read his maps while he ate and estimated Flagstaff was a solid two-day ride from his present location. After eating, he tested Boyle's legs.

Holding Boyle by the bit, Murphy walked backward and Boyle moved forward with a slight limp in the front left leg.

Murphy sighed and rubbed Boyle's neck.

"You won't make it," Murphy said.

He stuffed his pipe and sipped coffee as

he checked the maps again. About five miles to the south was listed as private land. It had to be a ranch. His only chance to catch Kyoto was to head for it and hope he could buy a new horse while Boyle recovered.

Murphy looked at Boyle.

"If we both walk, can you make five miles?"

Boyle snorted.

"Yeah, my feet hurt, too," Murphy said.

Close to sundown, Murphy, holding Boyle in tow, reached the fringe of the ranch he located on the map.

A wood sign was suspended across a gateway arch that led to a private, dirt road.

The sign read, **Clinton Ranch. Horses and Cattle.**

Murphy walked Boyle the quarter mile to the ranch house and arrived after dark. Lanterns illuminated the windows. Smoke rose up from the chimney. Several horses were in a corral opposite the house.

Murphy walked to the steps of the porch.

"Hello inside!" he called out.

Within seconds, a rifle appeared in a window.

"I mean you no harm," Murphy said. "My name is Murphy. I'm a US Secret Service Agent. My horse has a bad leg. Come take a look if you don't believe me."

Murphy heard the drop bar being lifted from inside and the door slowly opened. A man about sixty-years-old, holding a double-barreled shotgun, stepped out onto the porch.

"This is double-buck," he said. "And if that ain't enough to suit you, my son has a Winchester aimed at your gut."

"It's enough," Murphy said. "Are you Clinton?"

"I am. Christian name of George. My son is Isaiah. I'm coming down to take a look at your horse."

Clinton walked down the steps and stood in front of Murphy. "Tall fellow, ain't you," he said. "Got any government papers says who you say you are?"

Murphy dug out his flap wallet and held up his Secret Service identification.

Clinton nodded. "Let's take a look at your horse."

"Right front leg," Murphy said.

Clinton lifted Boyle's right front leg and carefully inspected in, then released it and looked at Murphy. "Muscle tear," he said. "Be at least a week before you can ride him."

"I need a horse," Murphy said.

"Come inside," Clinton said. "My missus

got supper ready."

Elizabeth Clinton, around her husband's age, was a handsome woman. She served a dinner of pot roast and Murphy thought it as good as any he'd had in the Washington restaurants.

Isaiah Clinton, the youngest son of three sons at nineteen, and the only one still living at home according to Clinton, was a tall, broad-shouldered young man and he sat to Murphy's left at the table.

"I can heal your horse, but it will take two weeks before he can support a man's weight," Clinton said.

"I'll need to buy or rent a horse to reach Flagstaff and possibly beyond," Murphy said.

"What do you mean rent?" Clinton asked.

"How much would a horse equal to Boyle cost to buy?" Murphy asked.

"Three-hundred dollars I'd reckon," Clinton said.

"I will give you three-hundred dollars to use a horse equal to mine and when I return you can have him back and keep the full three hundred," Murphy said.

Clinton looked at his son. "We have any like Mr. Murphy's in the pasture?"

"Yes, Pa," Isaiah said. "About two years old."

"We have a deal, Mr. Murphy," Clinton said.

"Good. Thank you."

"And you'll stay the night," Elizabeth said. "We have two extra bedrooms since our eldest boys moved away."

"Isaiah, right after supper, take Mr. Murphy's horse to the barn and give his leg a mustard plaster," Clinton said. "Use the liniment the vet gave us his last visit."

"Yes, Pa."

Elizabeth served coffee on the porch. Two wall-mounted oil lanterns illuminated the seating area.

Murphy stuffed his pipe and lit it with a match.

Clinton rolled a cigarette.

Isaiah looked at Murphy's Peacemaker.

"Are you a lawman?" he asked.

"Federal," Murphy said. "US Secret Service."

"Is that like a marshal?" Isaiah asked.

"Similar, but I work directly for the president," Murphy said.

"You must be after some bad people," Isaiah said.

"That's enough talk, son," Clinton said.

"Go see to Mr. Murphy's horse."

"Yes, Pa."

After Isaiah left the porch and entered the barn, Clinton said, "My son doesn't get off the ranch much, Mr. Murphy."

"He seems like a fine boy," Murphy said.

"When you're ready, I'll show you to your room, Mr. Murphy," Elizabeth said.

Murphy glanced around the bedroom and noted the clothes in the closet and shoes under the bed.

"We like to keep the rooms as they were for when our eldest boys come to visit," Elizabeth said.

"I'll try not to disturb anything," Murphy said.

"Goodnight, Mr. Murphy."

Right after breakfast, Murphy visited Boyle in the barn while Isaiah went to fetch the horse from the fields for Murphy.

Murphy rubbed Boyle's neck and fed him some sugar cubes.

"I'll be back for you as soon as I can," Murphy said.

Outside the barn, Isaiah and Clinton waited with a male horse nearly as large as Boyle. Murphy's saddle and bags were already on his back when Murphy counted out three-hundred dollars and gave the bills to Clinton.

"His name is Noah," Isaiah said.

"Good name," Murphy said.

Noah was nearly as tall and heavy as Boyle, had good lungs and endurance, and Murphy rode until midafternoon before taking a break.

He fed Noah grain before fixing a quick lunch. Afterward he rested a bit while he smoked his pipe and drank coffee.

Flagstaff was still a day and a half ride away and there was no sign of Kyoto's tracks. He could have changed direction and headed south or even north. There was no way to know if Kyoto went to Flagstaff except to go there and find out.

As he sipped his coffee and smoked his pipe, Murphy felt something tug at him. He didn't know what it was, but something wasn't right in his mind.

The feeling nagged at him the rest of the way to Flagstaff.

CHAPTER TWENTY-SEVEN

Flagstaff was a true boomtown. Since the railroad came to it, coupled with the cattle business and ranchers, the population swelled to nearly two-thousand residents, six thousand if you counted the surrounding county.

As with most western towns that had a railroad station, the depot and office were on the fringe of town at least a hundred yards from the nearest street.

The ticket office was empty except for the station manager and he was keeping busy by mopping the floors.

The manager looked at Murphy as he entered the office.

"Sorry, friend, but service has been suspended by authority of the president," he said.

"I'm looking for two men," Murphy said and flashed his identification.

"Mister, the first few days the railroad

shut down I had a hundred people or more come through here. The last few days I haven't seen a soul."

"These two men are Japanese," Murphy said.

"From Japan? Coming through here?"

"They're wanted men," Murphy said. "They want to catch a train to California."

"I'd remember Japanese," the manager said.

"Sheriff Perry in town?" Murphy said.

"Perry took a sheriff's job in California. He said the climate was better. I don't blame him. New sheriff is Diggs."

"Obliged."

Murphy left the office and walked Noah to town and found the sheriff's office on Main Street.

Sheriff Diggs, a large man of about forty, was writing in a log book when Murphy entered the office.

Murphy had his flap wallet out and set it on the desk to show his identification.

"Can I buy you a steak and a cup of coffee?" Murphy asked.

The restaurant located inside the Flagstaff Hotel served a decent steak and as Murphy and Diggs ate lunch, Murphy explained his business in town.

"I haven't seen any men like you described in town, ever," Diggs said. "If my deputies had they would have mentioned it to me."

"The last tracks were headed here," Murphy said. "But, that was four days ago."

"Could they have gone south to catch the railroad in Phoenix or Scottsdale?" Diggs asked.

"Could be," Murphy said. "I'll send a wire to both and ask to check it out."

"They could also be holed up somewhere close waiting for railroad service to resume," Diggs said.

"I thought of that," Murphy said. "It would take a hundred men months to search a territory this size."

"So he must be holed up somewhere close to monitor the railroad," Diggs said.

"It would appear so," Murphy said.

"After you send your telegrams, are you going to stay in town?" Diggs said.

"At least overnight," Murphy said.

"I'll alert my deputies."

"One more thing. Walk with me to the telegraph office," Murphy said. "I need to send the telegrams myself."

The hotel bed was comfortable enough and wasn't the reason Murphy couldn't sleep. Whatever was nagging at him escaped clarity and he couldn't put his finger on it.

Finally, exhaustion won out and he drifted off to a light sleep.

Murphy sat down to breakfast in the hotel dining room and ordered a full breakfast, starting with coffee.

He was on a second cup when Sheriff Diggs entered the dining room and joined Murphy at the table.

"Sleep good?" Diggs asked as the waitress brought him coffee.

"Fair," Murphy said.

"Leaving town?"

"I'm going to backtrack and see if I can pick up Kyoto's trail," Murphy said. "I'm using a horse I picked up at the Clinton ranch. Mine went lame and he's staying in their barn."

"I know the Clintons," Diggs said. "Nice family. Mr. Clinton and his three sons come to town every few weeks for supplies."

"I met the youngest boy, Isaiah," Murphy said. "I stayed in a bedroom belonging to one of their oldest boys."

Sipping coffee, Diggs paused and looked at Murphy.

"Youngest boy?" Diggs said. "Isaiah is the oldest and the other two live at home. The Clintons had children later in life."

Murphy stared at Diggs for a moment.

"Are you sure?" Murphy asked.

"Of course," Diggs said. "I'm new here, but I've been in the law business some fifteen years and I never forget names and faces. I've met the entire family. I believe my deputy bought a horse from them awhile back."

Murphy closed his eyes for a moment and what had been nagging at him became clear. A grown man might leave some personal items in his old room at home for the times that he visits, but the room Murphy spent the night in looked like it was still occupied.

Murphy opened his eyes.

"Is the Clinton place inside your jurisdiction?" he asked.

"Just outside by a couple of miles. Why?"

"Sheriff, I'm deputizing you with federal authority," Murphy said.

"Why?"

"I know where Kyoto is hiding," Murphy said.

CHAPTER TWENTY-EIGHT

Murphy and Diggs rode up to the Clinton ranch house shortly after noon. Smoke rose from the chimney.

"Somebody is home," Murphy said.

"Clinton! George Clinton, it's Sheriff Diggs from Flagstaff! Please step out to the porch!" Diggs shouted.

The curtains at the window parted and Clinton said, "That federal man Murphy is with you, I see."

"Come on out, George," Diggs said. "We need to talk."

"Come on in, the missus has lunch on the table," Clinton said.

Elizabeth served hot roast beef sandwiches and lemonade and then took a seat next to her husband.

"Where are your two youngest boys, Mr. Clinton?" Murphy asked.

Clinton looked at Isaiah. "You tell it, son.

You were there."

Isaiah looked at Murphy. "I didn't mean to lie to you, Mr. Murphy."

"Never mind that now, boy," Clinton said. "Just tell it."

Isaiah nodded. "Me and my brothers . . . James and Matthew . . . they're twins and just about to turn fifteen," he said. "We was . . . were rounding up stray ponies on the north plains and didn't see him until he was pointing a rifle at us. He said he would shoot us if we tried to run. He had this other fellow with him, the both of them strange looking, and the other fellow tied our hands with rope and then forced us to bring them home."

"I had no choice," Clinton said. "He had the rifle to my son's head and threatened to kill him if we didn't help them."

"Help them how?" Murphy asked.

"Hide them until the railroad resumes," Clinton said. "He said he would release my boys when they were safely on board a train west. I was to buy the tickets and give them to him and they would release my boys."

Diggs looked at Murphy. "Do you believe him?"

"No."

"Why would he harm my sons if I keep my word?" Clinton demanded. "Why?"

"You and your entire family can identify him," Murphy said. "And I don't think Kyoto fancies spending the rest of his life in an American prison."

Elizabeth placed her hand over her mouth and gasped.

"My boys. My twins," she cried.

"He won't harm them," Murphy said. "I can guarantee it. Mr. Clinton, where are they hiding?"

"We have a line shack a mile southwest of here," Clinton said. "We use it during roundup in the fall and spring. They took my boys there."

"Show us," Murphy said.

A thousand yards from the line shack, Murphy, Clinton, and Diggs dismounted and took cover behind some tall brush. Murphy used his binoculars to zoom in on the cabin.

"Smoke from the chimney," Murphy said. "Mr. Clinton, what about supplies?"

"I'm supposed to bring them some tomorrow," Clinton said.

Murphy examined the cabin and surrounding area. It was open country. Four horses were corralled in a small holding pen. A rider could be seen from a thousand yards in any direction.

Murphy lowered the binoculars.

"Let's go back to the house," he said.

Seated at the kitchen table, Murphy, Diggs, and Clinton drank coffee and waited for Elizabeth to join them after returning the pot to the woodstove. Holding a cup, she took a seat.

"Mr. Clinton, tomorrow when you bring them supplies you will tell Kyoto the railroad will run in six days," Murphy said.

"But, how is that possible? The notice said . . ." Clinton said.

"It will run," Murphy said. "He will ask you to buy four tickets. He will want your sons to travel with him as hostages to California. You will convince him to trade you for your sons."

"How?"

"Do you own a business-type suit of clothes?"

"My church clothes."

"You will tell him it's less conspicuous for them to travel as three businessmen than two Japanese men and two white boys," Murphy said. "Kyoto isn't stupid. He'll agree to that. In three days, you'll arrive at the cabin wearing your suit. You'll ride to the station with Kyoto, buy the tickets, and board the train. You will leave your sons at the cabin."

317

"My husband is no lawman, Mr. Murphy," Elizabeth said.

"He won't have to be," Murphy said. "Sheriff, I need twenty volunteers to act as passengers on the train. Men, mostly. They're to sit scattered about the four cars so Kyoto has plenty of room. Tell them each volunteer will be paid one-hundred dollars."

"I can arrange that, but what do we do?" Diggs asked.

"Have one of your deputies act as a passenger," Murphy said. "The other will shovel coal."

"And us?"

"You will run the train," Murphy said. "And I will collect tickets."

"I've never operated a train before," Diggs said.

"We'll have the engineer show you the basics before we go," Murphy said.

Diggs looked at Murphy, nodded his head, and allowed a tiny smile to cross his lips. "It could work."

"My sons and my husband . . ." Elizabeth said.

"Will be fine, Mrs. Clinton," Murphy said.

"Don't worry," Clinton said to Elizabeth. "Mr. Murphy seems to know what he's doing."

"Sheriff, I'll be staying the night and will

318

meet you in town in three days," Murphy said. "I'll need you to send a telegram for me. It's classified, so swear the operator to secrecy."

"I can do that," Diggs said.

Murphy looked at the old rifle that hung above the fireplace.

"Mr. Clinton, do you have ammunition for that Sharps rifle hanging there?" he asked.

Chapter Twenty-Nine

"I feel kind of sick to my stomach," Clinton said.

"If you need to vomit, do it now," Murphy said.

Clinton dismounted and got to his knees and vomited up the nice breakfast Elizabeth prepared for them. When he was done, he mounted his horse.

"Go on now, and remember to act as natural as possible," Murphy said.

Murphy dismounted as Clinton rode the fifteen-hundred feet to the cabin. He removed the Sharps rifle from the saddle sleeve, loaded a .50-90 round into it, and then dropped prone and watched Clinton ride to the cabin.

As Clinton arrived at the cabin, the door opened and Kyoto stepped out with a revolver to one of the Clinton boy's head.

"No need o' that," Clinton said.

"I decide what the need is," Kyoto said. "Did you bring the supplies?"

"See the two large sacks on my horse?" Clinton said.

Kyoto shouted in Japanese and Ito came out, stepped down to Clinton's horse, and removed the two sacks and carried them inside.

"I have news," Clinton said. "The railroad will resume service in six days."

"Are you sure?"

"I'm sure."

"How far to Flagstaff?"

"Day and a half in a hard ride."

"If you wish to see your sons safely home, you will buy four tickets and return here in two days."

"Three tickets," Clinton said.

Kyoto stared at Clinton. "Remember this gun to your son's head."

"Two Japanese men traveling with two small white boys will attract undue attention," Clinton said. "I will be your hostage in my boys' place. Three businessmen traveling together won't be as much noticed. Don't you agree?"

"Yes, I agree," Kyoto said. "But, on my terms. In three days you will bring a wagon with two horses and supplies for the trip. All of us will travel to the railroad. Once you buy the tickets, I will release your sons and you will come with me to California. Your sons will not say a word or I will kill their father. Do we agree?"

"Yes," Clinton said.

"And you, boy?" Kyoto said.

"Yes," the boy said.

"And in case you think a sharpshooter hiding in wait will save your sons, it won't," Kyoto said. "A cocked gun will be on them at all times until I am safely on board. Understood?"

"All I want are my sons," Clinton said. "I'm no fool."

"Good. Be here in three days," Kyoto said.

Clinton nodded to his son, turned his horse, and rode away.

Burke was at his desk when a White House runner knocked on the door and came in with a sealed telegram.

The envelope was marked **PRIORITY**. After the runner left, Burke opened the telegram.

To Burke White House Stop From Murphy Stop. Need railroad to run from Flagstaff west at ten am in four days. Stop. Kyoto will be on board. Stop More details to follow Stop Murphy

Burke read the telegram twice. "Son of a bitch," he said.

Then he stood up and went to see the president.

"A wagon doesn't surprise me," Murphy said as he mounted Boyle.

"But, will he keep his word and let my boys go?" Clinton asked.

"One is easier for him to watch than two," Murphy said. "I'll see you at the railroad station, Mr. Clinton. Keep your head about you and this will all work out."

"Would prayer help?" Clinton asked.

"It won't hurt," Murphy said.

Clinton nodded. "Ride him easy. That leg is still not a hundred percent."

President Arthur read the telegram and then looked at Burke, who stood before the Oval Office desk.

"What is he up to, Burke?" Arthur asked.

"It sounds very much like he has a trap planned for Mr. Kyoto."

Arthur nodded. "Do it," he said. "Whatever Murphy wants, do it."

CHAPTER THIRTY

Murphy looked at the twenty volunteers that stood on the platform at the depot.

With Murphy were Sheriff Diggs and his two deputies. Diggs was dressed as a railroad engineer. One deputy was dressed for shoveling coal. The second deputy wore the suit of a business traveler.

"The train should be here within the hour," Murphy said. "I expect Kyoto to arrive shortly after that. I would like fifteen of you to board as soon as the train arrives. The other five wait inside the ticket office. Remember to spread out so Kyoto has lots of room. Any questions?"

"If there's shooting?" a man asked.

"If you're in the car Kyoto is in, duck down behind your seat and wait it out," Murphy said. "In the other cars you probably won't even hear it."

In the distance, a whistle blew.

Murphy turned to Diggs.

"How do I look?" he asked.

Diggs inspected the railroad conductor suit Murphy wore. A tailor did a rush job on the pants length and even so, they were a bit too short for Murphy's height.

"Does it matter?" Diggs said.

"No."

Murphy and Diggs watched the station from the locomotive.

"When the train reaches fifty miles an hour, that's when I'll collect tickets," Murphy said. "If something goes wrong and he manages to slip away, he won't get far jumping from a train at that speed."

"Wagon's coming," Diggs said.

"Fire up the engine," Murphy said. He looked at the deputy. "Start shoveling some coal."

Clinton drove the wagon. Kyoto sat next to him. In back, Ito held a cocked revolver on his two boys, who were tied together with rope.

Clinton stopped the wagon behind the depot office and climbed down from the buckboard.

"If anyone but you returns, Mr. Ito will shoot your sons," Kyoto said.

Clinton nodded and then walked around

front and entered the office. Five people were in the office besides the man at the counter.

"It will be all right," the man at the counter said when he gave Clinton three tickets.

Clinton nodded, took the tickets, and returned to the wagon.

Kyoto stepped down and took the tickets from Clinton.

"Cut them loose," Kyoto said. "And you boys listen carefully. Ride home and say nothing to anybody or you will never see your father again."

Appearing as three businessmen, Kyoto, Ito, and Clinton boarded the train, along with five other passengers.

"Middle car," Kyoto said.

Kyoto, followed by Clinton and then Ito, boarded the middle car. Kyoto selected center seats away from the three other passengers on board.

"How long to reach California?" Kyoto asked Clinton.

"This is a limited stop train," Clinton said. "Thirty-six hours according to the schedule."

"Mr. Ito, you may see your family once again," Kyoto said.

Ito glared at Kyoto.

"And me, will I see my family again?" Clinton asked.

"If you do as you are told," Kyoto said.

"I love my family, Mr. Kyoto," Clinton said.

Kyoto nodded. "Good."

"Take her out, Sheriff," Murphy said.

Diggs spun a few dials and wheels and moved the throttle forward and the train rocked and slowly moved forward.

"The engineer told me it would take at least two miles to get her up to fifty miles per hour," Diggs said.

The station rolled by and after a few minutes, they were clear of Flagstaff and moving west on open track.

"Ten miles per hour," Diggs said. "Let's open her up a bit."

Diggs moved the throttle and Murphy watched the gauge move to fifteen and then twenty miles per hour.

"Deputy, strap on your gun," Murphy said. "You follow me, but stay in the car directly behind me."

The deputy put down the shovel and picked up his holster from the floor.

"Sheriff, you might want to put yours on, too," Murphy said.

"Hitting thirty-five," Diggs said and he picked up his holster from the conductor's seat behind him.

Murphy watched the gauge climb to forty, then forty-five, and finally fifty.

"Hold her right there, Sheriff," Murphy said.

"Good luck," Diggs said.

Murphy looked at the deputy. "Ready?"

The deputy nodded.

"Let's go," Murphy said.

Kyoto was in the middle car in a center aisle seat. Ito and Clinton sat opposite him. Murphy stood on the platform between cars and looked through the glass in the sliding door at Kyoto.

Murphy slid the door open and entered the car.

Kyoto gave Murphy a fleeting glance and saw the uniform and not the man. That gave Murphy the few seconds he needed to walk across the car, draw his Peacemaker, cock it, and aim it directly at Kyoto from the distance of one seat.

At the sound of the Peacemaker being cocked, Kyoto looked closer at Murphy and recognition set in and his eyes went wide.

"Don't even breathe," Murphy said.

"Stand with your hands in the air and do it slowly."

"Mr. Ito will shoot our hostage," Kyoto said.

"And then I will shoot you and Mr. Ito," Murphy said. "Because as they say in America, things happen in threes."

Slowly, Kyoto stood up and placed his hands on his head.

"I have immunity according to diplomatic law in your country," Kyoto said.

"It's been revoked," Murphy said. "The only question is which country you will rot in jail in."

"I don't think so, Mr. Murphy," Kyoto said. "You see, if I don't return to Japan inside a certain time frame, tens of millions of dollars of American counterfeit money will flood the European stock market. Soon after that, tens of millions more. Your economy will be in shambles inside of a year. America, the budding giant, will be reduced to an infant once again. So take me to Washington and let's discuss this with your president and his staff."

Murphy holstered the Peacemaker. "Help me to understand why you're doing this."

"In the last decade, your country has sent your Army to train the Japanese military on modern ways," Kyoto said. "We now wear western clothing, eat western food, and as a country we are losing who we are as a people. The samurai is no more. Soldiers with weapons purchased from America now protect the Emperor. I once sat in the Emperor's court and advised him on agriculture and beef, but now American businessmen do this, and their interests are America and not Japan."

"This is all about revenge?" Murphy asked.

"It's about losing my heritage to America, Mr. Murphy," Kyoto said.

"And Ito?" Murphy asked.

"Mr. Ito was a master engraver and designer at the Imperial Mint," Kyoto said. "It is amazing how talented a man he is, and even more amazing the lengths he will go to in order to save his family back in Japan."

"You have them hostage?" Murphy said.

"Let's say guests of my friends," Kyoto said.

"That's why when your men beat him they didn't touch his hands," Murphy said.

"You're very observant, Mr. Murphy."

"Sit," Murphy said.

Kyoto took his seat.

"Mr. Clinton, you can go," Murphy said.

Clinton stood, looked at Murphy, and then walked to the sliding door and opened it. As he stepped to the other car, the deputy entered and walked to Murphy.

"Deputy, tell the sheriff to take us back to Flagstaff," Murphy said.

The deputy nodded and turned around.

Murphy sat next to Ito and looked at Kyoto.

"Washington is very nice this time of year, isn't it?" Kyoto asked.

"Yes, it is," Murphy said.

CHAPTER THIRTY-ONE

Jack Harvey represented the Justice Department and spoke for President Arthur in the daylong meeting with Murphy and the Chief Marshal for the US Marshal's Service, Richard Jesse.

The meeting took place in a locked room in the Justice building in Washington.

"I understand how you feel, Murphy, but diplomatic relationships outweigh the benefits of prosecuting Mr. Kyoto," Harvey said. "In exchange for his freedom and passage home, he has given us the locations where all the counterfeit money is being stored. The Emperor's private police are busy confiscating it. In addition, Mr. Ito's family has been freed and is under the protection of the Emperor's personal bodyguards."

"I suppose it means nothing to the law that I have Kyoto's fingerprints on counterfeit bills he passed to banks out west," Murphy said.

"Oh, hell, Murphy," Jesse said. "Ninety-five percent of law enforcement never even heard of fingerprints."

"Kyoto will be dealt with by the Emperor himself when he is delivered to him by the US Marshal's Service," Harvey said. "And losing Kyoto to Japan is a far better outcome than a declaration of war, don't you think?"

"My men will be with Kyoto every second aboard the schooner on the way to Japan, Murphy," Jesse said. "He'll get his due, just not here."

"It's out of your hands, Murphy," Harvey said. "If it means anything to you, the president expresses his gratitude to you for what you've done."

Murphy stood up from the conference table.

"The president can kiss my ass," he said.

Harvey and Jesse stared at Murphy.

"I wasn't asking," Murphy said and walked out of the room.

"What do you mean you don't know where Burke is?" Murphy said to Burke's private secretary at his White House office.

"He left early this morning and said he had some business to tend to," she said. "He didn't say where or when he would return. I'm sorry, sir."

Murphy left the White House and walked to the private stables to retrieve Boyle. Clinton had done a first-class job of healing Boyle's leg and he showed no ill effects from the injury.

Murphy gave Boyle a few sugar cubes as he placed the saddle on his back.

"Let's go check the farm house and make sure it's locked tight, and then we'll catch a train to Tennessee and see Sally," Murphy said. "And then you can spend the rest of your days chasing the girls in the pasture."

Boyle turned his head and snorted.

"Yeah, we both got some chasing to do," Murphy said as he mounted Boyle and rode him out of the stable.

CHAPTER THIRTY-TWO

When Murphy turned off the dirt road onto his property, he was surprised to see Burke seated in a chair on the front porch. He was smoking a cigar and sipping whiskey from a glass.

Murphy dismounted and climbed the steps.

"What are you doing here?" Murphy asked.

A table with a bottle of Murphy's father's whiskey and a second glass was next to Burke. He lifted the bottle and filled the glass.

"We need to talk," Burke said.

Murphy took the chair at the table opposite Burke, lifted the glass, and took a sip. "What about?"

"Sally."

"What about Sally?"

"She's . . . gone, Murphy," Burke said.

Murphy stared at Burke for a moment.

"What do you mean gone? Gone where?"

"At least seven weeks now, and I don't know where."

"Why did she go?" Murphy asked.

"I can't say."

"Can't, or won't?"

"Murphy, she left of her own accord. You can't . . ."

Murphy was out of the chair in the blink of an eye, grabbed Burke by the jacket, lifted him up like a child, and held him so they were eye level.

"I will throw you off this porch, rope you like a steer, and Boyle will drag you through the north field until every bone in your body is broken," Murphy snarled. "Why did she leave?"

"Put me down, Murphy," Burke demanded. "I am your friend. Probably your only friend. Now put me down."

Murphy lowered Burke and Burke took his chair.

"Sit and listen," Burke said.

Murphy sat and picked up his drink.

"Sally was . . . violated," Burke said.

"Violated? You mean raped?"

"Yes."

"Who?"

"I got rid of him. That doesn't matter. What does matter is that she's . . . carrying his child and she told me she was leaving because she doesn't want you to commit murder. I don't know where she went. I give you my word on that."

"Who?"

"You can't take the law into your own hands on this," Burke said. "You'll be spitting on your whole life if you do."

"Who?"

"Murphy, listen to me for God's sake."

Murphy tossed back his drink and set the glass on the table. Then he stood, drew his Peacemaker, cocked it, and stuck it against Burke's skull.

"Who?" Murphy said, softly.

Burke closed his eyes.

"Christopher," Burke said.

There was a moment of silence.

Murphy de-cocked the Peacemaker and placed it into the holster.

"The carriage driver she gave lemonade to?" Burke asked.

"Yes."

"Where is he?"

"I swear I don't know."

"No matter," Murphy said.

He walked down the steps to Boyle and in one graceful motion was in the saddle.

"I'll find him," Murphy said.

Burke stood up and leaned against the

railing of the porch.

"How will you find him?" Burke said.

"Tell me, Burke, you never heard of Murphy's Law," Murphy said, and rode away.

ABOUT THE AUTHOR

Ethan J. Wolfe is a native of New York City. He has traveled and studied the American West extensively. He is the author of the novels *The Last Ride* and *The Regulator*.